Tempting Fate

S.A CLAYTON

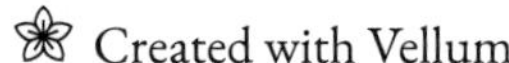
Created with Vellum

Author Note

Tempting Fate was originally published by Lady Boss Press in 2021. It is now being republished by me with names changed but all plot points are the same.

Prologue

JADE

What am I doing here?

As I step foot into Club Delirium, I look around. This is the one place I know I'll find him. The man who has consumed every passing thought since I was old enough to know what my feelings meant.

Gage Masterson.

He's been the epitome of perfection for me since my brother, Parker, brought him home one night after school. I've been lost in his emerald eyes ever since. Not that he's noticed—but I'm determined to change that tonight. I spent all of yesterday scouring my closet, looking for something that would turn his head. For a split second, I didn't think I had anything then I found this dress stashed in the very back of my wardrobe. Red, short, and a cleavage-revealer. I have no idea where it came from, but it's perfect for what I need tonight.

The air inside the club is thick as my eyes scan the room, taking in the men and women in various stages of undress—some on their knees, others bent over a person's lap, and a few tied and hanging from the ceiling. A sex club wasn't really on my list of things to experience at twenty-three, but before last week, I didn't even know this place existed. That was until I went on a blind date, only to be brought here. *Stunned* isn't an adequate description of what I felt when I came in here that first night. But seeing Gage? That pushed me over the edge. He's been gone for six years, left without a word—not that I expected one since I'm pretty sure he's never given me a second glance or thought.

Why are you here? I ask myself again, taking my time as I head toward the bar. As I walk up, Sal gives me that friendly grin I know makes all the girls fall at his feet.

"Hey there, darlin'. Didn't expect to see you back here so soon." I shrug my shoulders, my eyes scanning the area once more, hoping to catch a glimpse of Gage before he sees me.

But, of course, not.

"I decided to give it another try." He places a drink

in front of me. When I question him with my eyes, he taps the bar with his knuckles.

"On the house."

I say thanks and take a seat, trying my best to avoid every scene playing out around me. I can hear the moans of a few women, along with some masculine grunts, and the longer I sit here, the more aroused I become. Just as I'm about to down my drink, the air in the room changes, and the hairs on the back of my neck stand up as I hold my breath.

He's here.

"I didn't expect to see you here again," Gage whispers against the crook of my neck, causing goosebumps to travel across every exposed inch of my skin.

"You underestimated me, Gage," I mutter, eyes forward, trying my hardest not to let on just how turned on I am with him this close.

"You're in way over your head, little bug..." he warns, the nickname sending shockwaves through my body. His fingers grip my side as he spins me around, and the second his eyes land on mine, every snarky retort I had flies out of my brain, leaving me speechless. He looks even better than he did the other night —leather jacket pulled tightly across his broad shoulders, jet-black hair in direct contrast with his green eyes. And from what I can see through the tight black shirt, he's got enough abs to grace a romance cover.

He arches a brow as if waiting for me to say something, but I just turn around and grab my drink off the bar, taking a long swig. I hold back a cough as it burns all the way down.

"I should warn you, Sal is a very generous bartender..." His expression is one of amusement as he takes a step closer. I lean back. "What are you doing here, Jade?" he growls, the teasing light in his eyes gone in a flash as pure anger surfaces.

"Why do you care?" I ask, trying my hardest to seem flippant when in reality, all I want is for him to stay right where he is.

"I care because this place isn't for girls like you."

"Girls like me? You don't even know me. I'm pretty sure you've been gone for the past six years, so sorry if I don't give a shit what you think." I know I want him to see me as the woman he's always wanted, but I can't help the anger that rises when I realize that he probably still sees me as the little girl that used to follow him around like a lovesick puppy.

Before I can say anything else, he takes my hand and pulls me away from the bar, leading me from the main area to a back corner. Suddenly, he turns, fitting himself against the wall.

"What the fu—?" He interrupts me by spinning me around. Now facing the room, his hands land on my hips, pulling me flush against his chest.

"Look," he says against the shell of my ear. Arousal pools between my legs as I do exactly as he says. He points to a couple making out on the couch directly in front of us. The man reclines on the sofa, the woman straddling his legs, riding him as if they have no care in the world. "I want you to watch them. Don't take those gorgeous eyes off them."

My breath hitches as his fingers dig into my flesh, traveling past my hips to lightly brush my thighs. "You don't think I noticed how much you fucking grew up while I was gone?" he mutters against my shoulder, his lips parting as his tongue gently grazes my flesh. "You don't think I went home the other night and jacked off to the thought of what you would feel like wrapped around my cock, riding me like she's riding him?" I whimper, my gaze moving back to the couple on the couch, feeling a new surge of arousal shoot straight to my core.

"What?" I whimper, leaning my head back as his lips brush the crook of my neck. "*Gage...*" Reality obliterates every fantasy I had coming into this club as his fingers lift the hem of my dress, exposing the black lace thong I'm so glad I decided to wear.

“Don’t you dare take your eyes off them,” he growls against my skin as his fingers slip past the edge of my panties and delve into my flooding heat. “Jesus, you’re so wet. Parker’s gonna kill me for this.”

“Parker doesn’t have to find out.” My fingers grip his wrist, showing him the rhythm I love. When he chuckles against the side of my head, I sink deeper into him.

“Oh, you have no idea how I’m going to enjoy you,” he states, showing me how wrong all my fantasies were. Because Gage Masterson is better than anything I could have imagined.

Until he leaves.

CHAPTER 1

Jade

"A sex club?" I mutter, pulling my best friend Halley down the street and away from what I know is anything but a regular house.

"Are you insane?" I question, wondering where exactly she got the idea to come here and why she thought it was a good idea. An uneasy feeling creeps into the recesses of my mind because this isn't the first time I've been here. This isn't even the second. But Halley doesn't know that. And I really don't want to be standing in the middle of the street the first time she hears about it.

"Not just any sex club. *The* sex club in Seattle. Club Delirium." I roll my eyes because the excited look in hers lets me know that...one, my best friend is into things I never thought she was. And two, she has no idea that I've been here before.

"Halley, how did you find out about this place?" A part of me doesn't want to know the answer, but the other part is curious about how my straightlaced friend knows about a place like this. When she doesn't answer and instead looks at her phone and smiles, realization hits. *Ian*. Her new boyfriend.

"Please tell me you don't come here because of Ian." Her gaze shoots up, and guilt wafts off her in waves. I groan as I spin and walk away.

"Come on, Jade. I know it sounds crazy and like a bad idea." I give her the *you think* look before she takes one of my hands in hers and squeezes. "But Ian brought me here before and I honestly think you'll love it." Her pleading eyes are my kryptonite, and she knows it.

"Fine, " I mutter. She jumps up and down and then hugs me close.

We walk toward the front of the place when my heart suddenly starts beating wildly. I pray Nick isn't working the door tonight. He'll recognize me in a second, even though it's been years since I stepped foot into Club Delirium. Not since my whole world fell apart.

"Jade? You okay?" I snap myself out of my memories and glance at Halley, who looks concerned.

"Yeah, I'm fine, just nervous, I guess." The answer must satisfy her. She smiles, takes my hand in hers, and leads me closer to the front door. *Please don't be Nick, please don't be Nick,* I silently beg before Halley hits the doorbell, and footfalls echo behind the closed door. My heart continues racing, my hands beginning to shake as the sound gets closer and closer until it stops right in front of us. I don't mean to hold my breath, but I do as the door opens to reveal an enormous blond-haired, blue-eyed god covered in tattoos from head to toe. If I weren't so freaking relieved that he isn't Nick, I might be intimidated.

"Yes?" he questions as I let out the breath I was holding as Halley explains who we are. After a minute, he motions for us to enter, shutting the door behind us.

I take in the foyer, which looks like a typical house: hardwood floors, painted walls, and a doorway that I know leads to the main attraction. Before I have a chance to get my bearings, Halley leads me over the threshold and into the main room.

Deep-cushioned couches rest on the same hardwood floors that flow throughout the space. Red and brown chairs have been positioned in the corners, allowing for some privacy while still being out in the open. The lights above me are dim, making the atmosphere warm and inviting, and I instantly regret this decision. Why did I think it would be a good idea to return here when I know what this place means? When I know who it reminds me of.

"Baby..." Ian says with his arms outstretched as Halley falls into his embrace. The sight of them here, like this, sends me flying back to when this place was *my* safe place. When Gage and I were still...us.

"You nervous, little bug?" Gage whispers in my ear, his facial hair scratching the side of my cheek in a way that sends delicious tingles down the length of my spine. His tattoo-covered hands grasp me from behind and pull me against his hardened chest. It's only been a few weeks, but I'm addicted to him—to his touch, to his smell, and to the way he makes me feel so freaking alive.

"Should I be nervous?" His hands travel past my navel and stop at the clasp of my jeans.

"Little bug, you should always be nervous around me when you look so damn edible," he mutters, kissing up the side of my neck, nibbling the lobe of my ear. "And I know we've done this before, but I want to make sure you're okay..." He trails off, his breath hot against my skin as he deftly undoes the button on my jeans, then

pulls down the zipper before his fingers sink into my panties, causing my breath to catch.

"I want you to watch them," he demands as his other hand holds me tightly against him so I can feel what this is doing to him. "I want you to see what he's doing to her. Know that I will do the exact same thing to you later." I stare forward, taking in the couple before us, watching as the man ties up his submissive with care, dedication, and precision.

"Gage..." I moan as his fingers lightly trace over my sex, causing my hips to buck in response.

"Do you like what you see?" he asks, not putting pressure on the place he knows I love the most, yet still teasing me, toying with me. I bow my head, closing my eyes as the pressure inside me almost becomes too much.

"Eyes open, little bug. I don't want you to miss this." Just as the man finishes tying up his subject, he hoists her in the air, suspending her from the ceiling. "What I wouldn't do to see you like that, completely at my mercy, open and willing to take whatever I choose to give you."

"Jade?" Halley asks, taking my hand in hers and waking me from my memories. *Shit, I don't know if I can do this.* I give her a slight nod before her attention turns back to Ian as if she's conflicted.

"Go. I'll be fine," I say, pointing to the bar and giving her the best smile I can muster. It must work because she hugs me and then joins Ian, leaving me to deal with the remnants of the past I'm about to face.

CHAPTER 2
Gage

"So, you're finally home," Parker says as I head into my bedroom and open my closet. I knew he'd call. He's been texting me since my plane landed, wondering when I'd get home.

"Yes, I'm finally home. And also…I'm great by the way, thanks for asking." I can't hide the sarcasm as I take out a black t-shirt, dark-wash jeans, and black shoes.

"Yeah, yeah. Are we hanging out?" he asks. I chuckle, putting the phone on speaker as I get dressed.

"Sure, just not tonight. I'm starting my new job."

"Already? You just landed and you're already working? I thought joining the military meant you didn't have to do that when you got out?"

"Just because I left the military doesn't mean I don't need, you know...money." I hear his distant laugh as I pull my shirt over my head and look in the mirror. My jet-black hair hangs over my forehead, and my dark-rimmed glasses frame my green eyes. As much as Parker likes to describe me as a *pretty boy*, the tattoos that cover my entire torso and arms tell a different story.

"Fine, but you have to come over for drinks soon, I haven't seen you in years, man." I agree and hang up the phone. As much as I miss my best friend, I haven't seen him in years for a reason. The reason I joined the military and left on a red-eye without telling anyone to begin with. And that reason—*person*—has haunted my dreams since the day I left.

Jade.

As much as I knew that coming home would be difficult, being here, surrounded by memories of the woman who brought me to my knees, is slowly crushing me.

And it's only been a few hours.

I glance at the clock hanging from my bedroom wall and silently curse as I gather my things and head out the door, hoping I can leave the memories behind.

. . .

Temptation isn't a place I thought to see again. But a sense of familiarity hits when I walk through the door, gesturing to the bouncer as I cross the foyer and head into the main room. I smirk. I don't know why I expected it to look different after all these years, but when I see the dim lights, the couches, and the clusters of chairs, a sense of relief washes over me—as well as a bombardment of memories. The last time I was in this building, everything I thought I wanted blew apart.

"Little bug, you look edible tonight," I murmur against Jade's ear as I pull her closer, the smell of her perfume overtaking my senses. "You have no idea the things I want to do to you tonight. I even reserved a private room." Her eyes widen. It's a step we haven't taken. Although we're both open to trying new things, the rooms haven't been one of them. Yet. But from the fire in her eyes, I can see that she likes the idea.

"Honey." She moans, taking my hand and bringing it to her lips to kiss the palm, sending tingles straight to my dick. This woman drives me crazy, and if I don't get her into that room soon, I won't be responsible for my actions, and won't care who sees her getting her ass reddened by my hand. But the reason for us meeting here comes back to my consciousness, and I lean back against the bar, keeping my eyes on her.

"You asked to meet here for a reason I presume." I hope it's just because she can't get enough of me, or that she's been thinking about me as much as I've been thinking about her. But from the way she won't meet my eyes, and how tightly her fingers are twined together, I know it's the opposite. "Little bug, what's wrong?"

"I want to tell my brother about us." And just like that, it's as if a cold glass of water has been thrown in my face.

"You can't be serious. We said when we started this that he can't know. He'll kill me, Jade. You know that." Her gaze finally meets mine as a single tear falls from her eye.

"I know what I said. But I can't keep lying to him. He knows I'm seeing someone...he knows I'm..."

"He knows you're what?" I ask, knowing there's more she's not telling me.

"He knows that I'm falling in love."

"Gage! It's been a while, man," Sal says from behind the bar, shaking me out of my reverie. He's always been the light to my darkness. While I prefer my dark hair and darker clothes, he's the opposite with his blond hair, fair skin, and white t-shirts. If I remember correctly, the ladies seem to really enjoy him—unless things have changed since I left.

The place is packed, the atmosphere thrilling, but the adrenaline I once felt when I walked through the front door is gone. And I have a feeling I know why.

"Sal, good to see you." I hold out my hand as he takes it in his firm grip. "Honestly, I wasn't expecting you to still be here." I raise a brow as he gives me that signature smirk I know used to get him insane tips. From the look on some of the ladies' faces, I can tell it still works.

"Why leave a good thing?" The statement was likely meant to be a flash in the pan comment. But to me, it only reminds me what I ran away from and starts me wondering if it's possible to get it back.

"True," I mutter, heading into the locker room and putting all my things in my cubby before heading out onto the floor to start my shift. When I first decided to leave the military, I knew that finding a job would be hard since I had no idea what I wanted to do with the rest of my life. I've been so regimented for the last six years, figuring that out seemed daunting.

But Club Delirium has always been a safe haven for me. When I told the owner I needed a job to tide me over for a few months until I figured something out, he agreed to hire me on as a Dungeon Master. My sole purpose is to make sure that everyone is safe and that they're not being forced into something they aren't ready to experience. I'll also make sure the steady flow of drinks doesn't impede judgment—something I keep in mind as I circle the room, trying to keep my memories from taking over every time I see a couple in one of the stations set up around the room or just sitting on the couches, enjoying the show.

"Gage! Can you do me a favor?" Sal calls as I walk by, doing my rounds. I nod my head as I get closer. "Can you just watch the bar so I can take a leak? I shouldn't be too long."

"Sure, man. Take as much time as you need." He pats me on the shoulder as he passes, leaving me with a female bartender who seems to be busy flirting with one of her patrons at the end of the bar. I attempt to look happy as I spend the next few minutes trying to remember drinks I learned to make in college as I take care of as many people as possible.

"You new here, sugar?" an older woman says with a lustful look that would likely tempt any other man in the club. I look around, hoping she's with someone, but from the glint in her eyes, I know she's not.

"What can I get you, darlin'?" I use the term of endearment Sal always uses since it seems to work for him. But from the way she leans forward, showing off ample cleavage, I realize I might have made a big mistake.

"Apple martini." Her teeth rake over her bottom lip as her eyes scan my chest. Only one person ever affected me with that move, and she's not here.

Not anymore.

"Coming right up," I say with the best smile I can muster. It doesn't take me long to remember how to make the apple martini, and when I hand it to her, and our fingers brush, she winks.

"See you around, sugar." She takes a sip and walks away, allowing me to let out a relieved breath. I'm no stranger to women hitting on me, but turning down a paying customer is something I haven't gotten used to yet.

Just as I'm about to go looking for Sal, I feel the air in the room change, it becomes thick, heavy, and all-consuming. I lean against the bar, my back facing the room as I close my eyes, racking my hands through my short hair, hoping the overwhelming feeling sinking into my chest disappears.

"Excuse me? Can I get a drink?" The second that voice washes over me, I curse God or whoever put me behind this bar.

I would know that voice anywhere.

It's the voice that's haunted me for the past six years.

The one that belongs to my best friend's little sister.

"Jade?"

CHAPTER 3
Jade

This can't be happening. There is no way that Gage is standing in front of me, behind the bar of the sex club we used to come to *together*, staring at me like he's seen a ghost. If anything, he should be running away before I gouge out his eyes with the little umbrella lying on the bar beside me.

"Gage? What the hell are you doing here?" The accusation in my tone can't be missed, but the uneasy feeling creeping up my spine makes me question whether I want to punch his gorgeous face or kiss it. *Why does he have to look even better now than he did six years ago?* He definitely filled out. Those arms certainly weren't that big the last time they wrapped around me. The tattoo collection has gotten a lot more extensive, too. And from the looks of it, that smile of his is still as devastating as it was when I stupidly fell in love with him.

"What am *I* doing here? I could ask you the same thing!" His bright green eyes search mine, but I avoid them, knowing the effect they have on me, and not wanting to fall into the same pattern as we did before. Because that only left me with a broken heart and no one to turn to. "Does Parker know you're here?" he accuses. I chuckle under my breath at the mere idea of my brother knowing anything about this place.

"Parker doesn't know a lot of things," I mumble as I search the room, trying not to feel the longing in my chest, the desire for things to go back to the way they were before I knew the touch of his fingers against my skin, or the way his mouth could bring me more pleasure than I even imagined. But really, I just want things to go back to before I knew what loving Gage felt like. Because in this place, staring at his face, surrounded by the memories we made...it's a torture I never knew could feel so devastating.

"You know what, Gage? I can't do this. I'm leaving," I say, picking up my purse from the seat beside me and adjusting my dress as I make my way to the front door. Before I have a chance to make a break for it, Gage is in front of me, blocking my way.

"Gage, please move," I beg, keeping my eyes trained on his shoes, knowing that if his eyes land on mine, I'll do something I'll regret.

"No. I'm not letting you leave before you tell me why you're here." When I don't answer, he takes his fingers, places them under my chin and lifts until his gorgeous green depths are locked on mine. My stomach somersaults. *I am in so much trouble.*

"I hate to break it to you, Gage, but you don't have a right to any of that information anymore. You threw that away the second you ran from me...from *us*." I push past him, needing to get away from the heat of his body, away from the overwhelming scent of his cologne. Just away...from the man I know I could fall madly in love with again.

And I can't let that happen. Though truth be told, I don't think I really ever stopped.

"You know what would have happened if I'd stayed. You know it would've..." The anger in me starts to surface as I lift my head.

"It would've...what? Made things worse? Made Parker hate you? Hate me? What? What would have been so bad that you couldn't stay and fight for us?" Emotions well up behind my eyes, tears forming as I shake my head, trying to get myself under control.

"It would have destroyed your relationship with

your brother, and I couldn't be a part of that. I couldn't be the *reason* for that." His hand lifts as if he wants to touch me, but I back away.

"That wasn't your call to make, was it? I loved you. I was willing to risk my relationship with my brother because I couldn't stand the thought of losing you. Obviously, I wasted my time." I turn and walk out the front door, waiting for him to follow. When he doesn't, I take a deep breath and tell myself it's for the best. Gage is in the past. Something I learned from and can't revert to, because that only leads to trouble.

As I walk, my phone rings. Taking it out of my purse, I see it's Halley. "Where are you?" she asks as I stop, leaning back against a light post, silently berating myself for leaving without telling her I was going. I was so hung up on seeing Gage that I completely forgot that she was still with Ian.

"Fuck, Hal. I'm so sorry. I just needed to get out of there..." She takes a deep breath and whispers something to Ian, who I assume is right next to her.

"Thank God. Jade, we were looking everywhere for you!" Shit, I'm a horrible friend. "Are you okay?" Am I? I feel as if my entire world has been ripped out from under me again, causing me to slip back into the darkness I spent the last six years trying to escape.

"I'm fine. I'm just going to head home," I say,

hoping she doesn't notice the hitch in my voice or how I'm fighting back tears.

"Are you sure? I can have Ian drive you."

"No, that's okay. I need the air."

"Okay. Well, text me when you get home so I know you're safe." I tell her I will and start walking again, cursing the high heels I decided to wear instead of the flats I knew would be more comfortable. Just as I'm about to take off my shoes and say *"fuck it"* and go barefoot, I hear a honk beside me. When I turn my head and see Gage's Mustang, I curse whoever is playing this sick game because it's not funny anymore.

"Go home, Gage. I don't want to talk to you," I say as I continue walking as he drives creepily slow next to me.

"I know. But please let me drive you home."

"Don't you have to work?" I question, hoping he just leaves and goes back to the club.

"I got someone to cover for me. I told them I'd be back soon."

"And they were okay with that?" I quirk an eyebrow as I continue to walk down the street.

"Let's just say the owner and I are old friends..." He winks and I remember the fact that Gage used to be one of their best customers. "I know those shoes can't be comfortable, and it would make me feel better." I start laughing as I halt and turn toward the street, just as he stops the car.

"Oh, it would make you feel better? What about what I want, Gage? Did you ever think about that? Of course, not. If you did, you wouldn't have left me with only a note on my nightstand, telling me you were breaking up with me. So, excuse me if I don't give a flying fuck about your precious feelings." Just as I turn and start walking again, the heels I just spent the last ten minutes cursing decide they've had enough. One snaps in two, leaving me crumpled on the ground. To make matters worse, Gage gets out of his car and rushes to my side, picking me up and setting me next to the passenger door.

"I know you hate me," he mutters against my ear as I close my eyes and try not to remember what his hands feel like against my skin. "And you have every right to. But right now, I just want to make sure you get home safely."

I start to shake my head, but his fingers grip my hips, halting the movement and every thought I had. "Jade, I am not leaving you here to walk home alone in the middle of the night. I know you think I don't care about you, but you're wrong. So wrong. Please just get in the car. *Please.*" I sigh loudly, rolling my eyes, my antics causing a slight smirk to cross his gorgeous face.

"Fine. But I'm not going to enjoy it," I mutter, secretly loving the chuckle that rumbles through him.

It doesn't take long to get to my place. When Gage pulls up in front of my place and shuts off the car, I sit there wishing I were anywhere else. His vehicle still smells the same. And if I peer into the back seat, memories of our stolen nights will surely come flooding back, and I don't know if I can take another minute of being this close to him.

"What are you thinking about?" Gage asks, his head leaning against the headrest, his eyes looking forward.

"Nothing," I mutter, hoping the heavy feeling in my chest will leave the second I'm out of this car.

"Don't lie to me, little bug." I suck in a breath the second the nickname leaves his lips. I haven't heard that since the day he left, and the dominant tone in his voice causes something in me to snap.

"How dare you?" I spit in his direction as his eyes meet mine. "You have no right to call me that after what you did. And don't you use that tone with me again, because I will make you regret it." Before he has a chance to respond, I'm out of the car and walking toward the front door.

"Jade!" Gage yells as his footsteps creep up behind me. "I'm sorry. It just came out. I know I have no right, but you have to know that leaving you was the hardest decision I have ever made. And the one I regret the most." His fingers lightly grasp my wrist, causing my breath to catch. The feeling of his skin on mine is almost euphoric. *God, why did being around him have to be so tempting*? As I turn around, and our eyes meet once more, everything changes. The past melts away, and all I see is the man I loved with all my heart all those years ago. All I want is to feel his lips on mine one more time. So, before I think better of it, I reach up and grasp his neck, pulling his mouth to mine. The second I get a hint of that familiar taste, I groan.

Yup, I am in so much trouble.

CHAPTER 4

Gage

I shoot up, sweat pouring off me as if I ran a mile. Nope. Just reliving last night, that fucking kiss, and the fact that after sealing her lips to mine, Jade ran back inside her house and left me alone, wondering what the hell had just happened.

One minute I was baring my soul, explaining that what'd happened six years ago was nothing compared to what I put myself through after I left. And then the next minute, she was kissing me, And the next minute, she was kissing me. It pulled me into a sensation that couldn't compare to what my mind conjured up all those lonely nights away from her. It was way better.

My hands rub against the days' worth of scruff along my jaw as I try and process what the hell happened and where we go from here. Obviously, she feels the same pull I do, the one I felt surge through my entire body the second I saw her leaning against the bar. What I can't figure out is why she was at Temptation to begin with. *Has she been going without me?* I shake my head, knowing that's impossible. Jade was adventurous, but only with me. Before me, she was as vanilla as they came. But the second I introduced her to the club, everything changed. I watched her flourish and evolve into a sexy-as-hell woman who kept me on my toes and caused more than one sleepless night.

Before I allow myself to sink into the memories that are bound to cling to my skin all day long, I get out of bed and head into the shower, turning the knob until the water is scalding, hoping it will chase away the past.

It doesn't.

I spot her across the room and grin, loving the anticipation that crawls across my skin at the thought of touching her, tasting her, and feeling her wrapped around me. She knows I'm here—I texted her when I was outside—but she hasn't noticed me yet. And, honestly, I like it this way. Her jet-black hair is pin-straight, draped over one shoulder in the way she knows drives me crazy. She's wearing a black lace dress and bright red lingerie that peeks through the fabric. It's enough to drive me insane.

The closer I get, the stronger her scent becomes, and although I smell a hint of the perfume I gave her for her birthday, it's mostly just her. I growl low in my throat, loving how her body tenses when she hears the sound. She doesn't turn around; she knows better than that. But she does down her drink, placing the empty glass on the bar top for Sal to pick up later.

"You ready, little bug?" I murmur against her neck, my tongue tasting the saltiness of her skin. She doesn't move, but her breathing becomes uneven. One of my arms wraps around her waist, pulling her against my chest. "Answer me," I demand.

"Yes, I'm ready." The smirk that forms grows into a full-on smile when she turns, and I get the full impact of the woman in front of me. Fuck me, she's every man's wet dream, and I know exactly what I'm going to do with her.

"On your knees, little bug." Her eyes flare as my fingers grip her hips with some pressure, letting her know not to test my patience. At first, she doesn't move, but after a second, the smile I love so much captures my attention as she licks those lips that could bring even the strongest man to his knees.

"You want my mouth, baby?" She lowers herself, not caring one bit about the room full of people surrounding her, or the fact that the man sitting right next to her has

his eyes on her fingers as she expertly undoes my belt. Her eyes meet his, then mine as she winks, taking her time taking out my cock that hardens even more the second her dainty fingers wrap around its girth.

"Shit, little bug, you're killing me." I groan as her eyes meet mine one more time before she lowers her head, her hot breath cascading over my sensitive flesh, causing waves of pleasure to rocket throughout my body. Before I catch my breath, her mouth wraps around my cock, pitching me forward, my hands gripping the bar behind her. Jesus, her mouth feels fantastic.

"You love that people are watching, don't you? You love that they all wish they were me right now." She dips her head, taking a breath before swallowing as much of me as she can. Just as I'm about to tell her to stop, that I'll get us a private room, I watch as her free hand drifts down and under her dress, her body shuddering as she starts fingering herself. Everything around us disappears —the room full of people, the man I know is still watching, and the fact that every part of me wants to pull her up and fuck her against the bar.

I can't stop. Not when the feel of her hot, wet mouth surrounds me. And not when her fingers work her pussy. Just as a warm feeling grows at the base of my spine, I grip her arm. I take the fingers that were just inside her heat and place them in my mouth, groaning at the taste.

My woman is so turned on, sucking me off in front of everyone.

"Please, Gage, I need to come," she begs, tugging her hand from my grip. But I'm stronger and keep my hold.

"Do you deserve to come, little bug? Maybe I need a little more convincing..." Before I have the chance to tease her more, her mouth is back on my cock. She sucks harder than she ever has before, and everything starts to turn black. My grip loosens on her wrist, and she immediately starts stroking her clit as I grip the back of her head, making sure I'm as deep as I can get before I come down her throat. Not long after, she shudders with her own orgasm.

The memory blasts through me as the water splashes over my body. Before I can control it, hot, wet streams of cum coat the shower wall, leaving me breathless yet unsatisfied.

Shit.

I need to see her. I don't care if she's pissed at me. I don't care if I have to wait outside her door for three days straight. I will get her to talk to me. That memory sealed it for me. I am not going another day without that woman in my life.

Damn the consequences.

CHAPTER 5
Jade

"So, you're telling me that you kissed him and then just ran back inside? Like didn't even stay to see what his reaction was?" Halley asks. I shake my head, taking another long swig from the glass of wine she placed in front of me.

"I'm pretty sure I know exactly how he felt since it was directly against my stomach…" Her eyes widen as I shake my head. Why was I so freaking stupid last night? Why did I think that kissing Gage would make all the feelings inside me disappear? All it did was make me want him more. And it didn't help that every dream I had last night replayed every memory we made all those years ago. Or that I woke up so turned on that I had to take out my vibrator and get myself off before heading into the shower.

I spent all day at work trying to think of anything but the fact that Gage was back home, and that our chemistry was still as palpable as it was the day he left. I'm still incredibly pissed—no matter how much my body still wants him.

"Why didn't you ever tell me about him?" Halley asks. I'd spent the last hour trying to avoid this conversation altogether, but my best friend is persistent. "And why didn't you tell me you'd been to the club before? If I'd known what happened there, I wouldn't have brought you." I give her a knowing look because she's a big fat liar. When Halley wants something, she goes for it, and that includes begging, pleading, and blackmailing me to the point of concession. "Fine, but I would have stayed with you a bit longer..." she says. I choke on my wine, coughing into my arm as her gaze meets mine, the smile reaching her eyes.

"Halley, honey, I know you think you would do that, but when Ian's around..." I do a lewd gesture with my hips, and she hits me upside the head with a throw pillow. "Hey! I only speak the truth," I say through endless laughter as she leans back again and sighs.

"So, what's your plan?"

"My plan?" The corner of her mouth kicks up in a grin. "I plan to sit on this couch and drink this whole bottle of wine with you until I'm drunk enough to sleep a dreamless night and wake tomorrow to let future Jade deal with all this shit."

Halley rolls her eyes as she turns on the couch and faces me. The look on her face tells me she wants to ask me something but doesn't know how. I have a feeling I know exactly what she's going to say. "Go ahead. I know you want to ask," I prompt, filling my glass once more and leaning my head against the couch to gaze up at the ceiling.

"I…I don't really know how to ask it," she says nervously. I sit up straight and stare at the TV playing a rerun of *Friends*.

"You want to know how I started at Temptation and why I stopped going." I look over just as she avoids my eyes. Taking a deep breath, I prepare myself for the flood of memories. "Gage is Parker's best friend." Halley's eyes widen slightly, her glass pausing on its way to her mouth. "Yeah. And I had a crush on him since before I knew what crushes were." It's hard to describe how much I was obsessed with Gage growing up. He and Parker were inseparable, and I became a lovesick puppy, following them around until high school, when I realized very quickly how uninterested Gage was in his best friend's little sister.

"Nothing happened until after I came home from

college. I planned to stay at home until I could figure something out. One night, I went on a blind date and...he took me to the club."

"No way!" she shrieks as I laugh.

"I saw Gage there. He still looked as edible as he did back in high school, only older, sexier, and a lot harder to stay away from."

"Did he recognize you?"

"At first, no, but it didn't take him long." My breath shudders through my chest at the memory of that night. It was like a drug I never knew I needed. Sex for me had always been good, but I knew something was missing, a part of the experience that would make it go over the top. The second I walked into that club and looked around, I knew I had found it.

"So, he was there?" Halley asks, her wine forgotten as she leans forward like the story I'm about to tell is the only reason she's still breathing.

I nod because there's really no way I can explain what my body did when I saw him lounging on that couch with a woman between his legs, sucking on his cock as he talked to the man sitting beside him as if nothing were happening. Every once in a while, he would place his hand on her head, pushing in deeper, urging her to go faster. Either way, I stood there for way too long until his wide eyes met mine.

"He was pissed that I was there. Told me I had to leave, but I didn't."

"I bet he loved that..." She whistles, picking up her glass again to take a sip. "From what I've heard, the man loves control."

"You have no idea. He's a Dom, Halley. Which means when you're with him, he has complete control."

"And you liked that? It turned you on, not being in control?" I tilt my head to the side and think. No one has ever asked me that question. To be fair, no one really knows that part of my past, so those types of questions never come up.

"It wasn't the idea of losing control that turned me on," I admit. "It was the fact that this man wanted to do everything in his power to make me feel good...feel wanted. Even if that meant me doing exactly what *he* wanted." I actually shudder at the memory.

"But isn't that dehumanizing? Allowing someone to force you to do whatever *they* want?" I shake my head, giving her a small smile because this is exactly why I never told anyone. They always go for the worst-case scenario. When in reality, it's the opposite.

"Actually, allowing someone to make those choices for you is incredibly freeing. And you have to remember that every relationship is different. Some are more intense than others."

"Like Christian Grey." I roll my eyes because whenever someone even thinks about BDSM, they go straight to that character, a representation of a very specific type. When, in fact, there are *so* many more iterations.

"Kind of. I mean, he's a sensationalized version. But for Gage and me, we were more...vanilla. Inside the club and the bedroom, he was in charge. But as a couple? We were normal...until everything fell apart." Just thinking back to the day he left—or rather the day I found the note that told me he wasn't coming back—hollows out my stomach to the point where I have to take a deep breath and close my eyes, reminding myself that it's over.

"What happened?" Halley asks, and from the look in her eyes when our gazes meet, she knows it's not pretty.

"I wanted more. I was falling in love with him..."

"He left because you were in love with him?" she asks, clearly confused. I shrug my shoulders.

"Maybe. He could have also left because I wanted to tell my brother about us." Her whole body recoils.

"Parker didn't know?"

I shake my head as I drop my forehead into my

hands. “We wanted to keep it a secret because we knew how Parker would react. I knew from the moment we started that my brother would do whatever he could to sabotage the relationship. So, we kept it under wraps, snuck around, only stayed at Gage’s place because I was still at my parents’.”

“But then it changed for you?” I don’t have to say anything because she knows the answer. Of course, I thought it was mutual. That we had been together long enough that it wouldn’t matter what Parker said. But Gage proved me wrong.

“After I asked if we could tell Parker, everything changed. He ignored me for a few days. I even called Parker, asking if he’d seen him because I was worried. After that phone call, I knew what was happening. But I wasn’t sure until I found the letter on my nightstand.”

“He didn’t even break up with you in person?” I shake my head, the anger gone, replaced by a sense of emptiness that I fought to keep at bay for six years. But now that I’ve seen Gage again...it’s back.

“So, after that, I stayed away from Temptation because every wall, room, and person reminded me of Gage and what he did to me.” Halley says nothing as a knock sounds. We both look at each other, neither of us expecting anyone. I get up from the couch and place my glass on the table as I head toward the front door.

When I open it, Gage is standing there looking sexy as hell in a leather jacket that covers a black shirt, dark-washed jeans, and Converse shoes with his hair a mess. I pinch myself, flinching at the contact.

"What did you do that for?" Gage asks, his expression one of confusion.

"Making sure this isn't a dream," I mutter. His smile lights up his face as I take a deep breath. The sight of him is still something to behold.

"Hello, little bug." His eyes are deadly, and for the first time since he left, a sliver of hope gathers at the base of my spine, tingling and coming alive with every pass of his eyes. I know I told him not to use that nickname anymore, but the combination of his gaze and that dominant tone makes me putty in his hands. And he knows it.

Is this a good idea?

Probably not.

But right now, I don't care.

CHAPTER 6
Gage

She looks gorgeous in her plaid pajama pants and oversized white shirt. Her mass of black hair is tied in a knot on the top of her head, and my eyes can't stop taking her in. Her nipples are visible through the thin fabric of her shirt, and I have to mentally tell my dick to calm down because he apparently didn't get the memo that, right now, I just need to get into this house. After that, I can try and convince her to finish the kiss the way I've been dreaming about doing since I saw her last night.

"Can I come in?" I ask, hoping she doesn't slap me. But when she steps aside, I smirk. Knowing I still have some power over her like I used to is a good sign.

"Gage, I'm guessing?" a woman who I assume is Jade's roommate says as she gives Jade a wide-eyed look. I briefly watch as they have a silent conversation I'm not privy to and take the time to look around the room. It's small, a light blue couch situated beneath a large window, and a small TV sitting on a stand just opposite it. The walls are a bright yellow that flows right into the open-style kitchen that is way too small for me but looks adorable with Jade's rustic decor.

"Well, I see I'm probably just going to get in the way. I'm off to Ian's," the roommate states, looking back at me with narrowed eyes. "You hurt her in any way, and I will rip you apart, starting with your balls." I flinch at the insinuation but then give her a small smile.

I like her.

"I promise, I won't hurt her," I say, giving the Boy Scout salute as she rolls her eyes and mutters something about men making promises they can't keep, then shuts the door behind her as she leaves.

"You were never a Boy Scout," Jade mutters as she locks the door behind her friend, and we're left in agonizing silence.

"So, she seems lovely..." I tease, needing her to say something, *anything* to break the awkwardness surrounding us.

"What are you doing here, Gage?" Her voice is stern, but I can hear a sliver of nervousness, too. It's that emotion I cling to. Because I know if she's nervous, it's not something caused by fear or hatred. It's because of desire. And I can work with that.

"I think you know why I'm here, little bug."

"I told you not to call me that. You lost the right to use that name, remember?" As much as I want to believe her, the way her pupils dilate when I say the name, and the way her fingers clench at the mere sound of it tells me she's still affected. That the memories we made all those years ago still haunt her, just as they do me.

"Why did you kiss me?" I ask blatantly. When she averts her gaze and walks toward the couch, I clasp her wrist and spin her, bringing her chest against mine. "I don't want to have to ask again, little bug. Why did you kiss me?" Her breath is shallow as her gaze roams my face, searching for something, though I can't put my finger on what. As I wait for her answer, I lean down, my breath cascading over the sensitive flesh of her neck as I whisper, "You missed me that much?"

I don't feel the slap until she pulls away from me and yells, clasping her hand against her stomach. "Why don't they tell you how much that hurts?" she cries, wiggling her fingers as the pain in my cheek finally registers.

"Fuck!" I curse. I knew she was pissed at me, but to

actually hit me? I wasn't expecting that. "Jesus, Jade, what the hell was that for?" I murmur, rubbing the sensitive area and watching anger rise to the apples of her cheeks in the form of a blush.

"What was that for? Are you seriously asking me that right now?" Apparently, I don't answer quickly enough because she comes storming over, tears filling her eyes. And for the first time since walking in here, my stomach sinks to the floor in agony. "You *left* me, Gage. You knew how I felt, you knew that, and you still left me...alone." I start to shake my head, but she continues. "You disappeared into thin air as if those months meant absolutely nothing to you." That's all I can handle before I take her cheeks in the palms of my hands and hold her gaze.

"You think you meant nothing to me? You think that I didn't think about you every second of every day I was away from you? Jesus, Jade. I was in love with you, too!" She opens her mouth to say something, but I kiss her instead, sealing my lips to hers as she sinks into me, wrapping her arms around my neck as she pulls me close.

"Don't you dare think you're off the hook," she murmurs against my lips as I take her harder, pushing her against the closed front door. "I hated you for so many years..." Her voice breaks, and everything around us stops. I dip my head, taking her lips in a kiss so gentle it takes her breath. After, she lifts her eyes to mine.

"I'm sorry, little bug. I thought it was my only option." She shakes her head, tears beginning to fall as I wipe them away one by one, only stopping for another kiss. "I promise we will talk, but I can't have you pressed against me and concentrate on anything but you out of that t-shirt." Her fingers dig into my sides, pulling me closer as her hips lift to meet mine. "Shit, little bug, I can't stop this once we start. You either halt us right now, and we sit and talk on that couch of yours. Or we stay right here and start all the things I've been fantasizing about for six years." Before I utter another word, her lips are sealed to mine. If that's not an invitation, I don't know what is.

"You remember the rules?" I ask, sucking the sensitive skin of her neck as her hips buck against mine, and my hands find purchase on her ass, pulling her even closer. Her slight acceptance isn't enough, and she knows it. With a hand on the nape of her neck, I pull her away from my chest so our gazes meet. I see her hooded lids and the desire flaring in the depths of her eyes. "You forgot rule number one, little bug. Verbal. Answers. Always," I say, spinning her, her hands coming up to brace against the wooden door. My teeth sink into her shoulder, and her intake of breath leaves my cock wanting more.

"Yes, I remember..." she whimpers as I softly kiss the spot I just bit, licking up the side of her neck and sucking lightly on the flesh below her ear.

"Good girl." The shiver that goes through her body sends pleasure straight to my cock. It jumps at the thought of what's in store. "It seems your body missed me," I say as my fingers trace the edge of her oversized shirt, pulling the material up to expose enough skin to cause her breath to catch.

I've dreamt about this moment, the time when she'd give in to me again. And it's glorious. "You miss me, little bug?" I whisper into the shell of her ear as her head falls back, resting against my shoulder as one of my hands wraps around her middle, pulling her tighter against my hard cock. When she doesn't answer, I take hold of her hair that's slowly escaping its bun and let it flow past her shoulder, groaning at the familiar scent of coconut that fills my lungs. "Jade..." I warn, pulling her hair to the side, exposing her neck and attacking it the way I did just minutes earlier, causing her knees to buckle.

"Gage..." she whimpers, and my grin can't be stopped. My name on her lips is my biggest weakness, and she knows exactly what she's doing as her fingers dig into the wrist now descending lower and lower. "Please..." she begs, and my hand stops.

"Was that begging, little bug?" She vehemently shakes her head, but I know what I heard. "You know the rules, baby. On your knees." She whimpers again, her body shaking as I turn her, pushing her against the wall, caging her between my body and the drywall as my lips descend on hers.

Fuck.

This is bliss, and the way her mouth attacks mine the second our lips touch tells me all I need to know. Her body molds to mine as my fingers grip her with a ferocity I didn't know I possessed. Her arms wrap around my neck, and her teeth sink into my bottom lip. As her center meets my hardness, she whimpers, and I pull myself away, watching as her eyes slowly open.

The desire that mirrors what I feel causes every muscle in my body to relax. This is what I've been missing these last six years. Jade. It was always her.

"On. Your. Knees."

CHAPTER 7

Jade

I knew what I was doing the second the word left my mouth. *Please* was never something he allowed me to say. He always told me that he would know exactly when I was permitted pleasure—not a second before. And begging for it was never an option. And if I did? I'd spend the rest of the night on my knees until he told me otherwise.

I can't fight the flutter in my stomach as I descend toward the hardwood floor, wincing at the pain in my knees.

"Here," he says, taking off the leather coat that's been covering his gorgeous shoulders and handing it to me. The tattoos that peek out from under his shirt cause my breath to hitch, and I can't wait to trace every one of them with my tongue.

"Thank you," I say, taking the jacket and placing it under my knees, feeling instant relief. This is what I missed: the fire and ice that made him so compelling when we were together. Gage loves to be in control, and I love giving it to him. But that control has never meant me being in pain, uncomfortable, or pressured into doing something I don't want to do.

Never.

"Better?" he asks, his eyes boring into mine as I look up, wondering if this is real. When I say "yes," he flashes me a cocky smirk. "Do you know why you are on your knees, Little Bug?" I nod, but he shakes his head. "I need the words, sweetheart."

"I begged..." I admit. He motions for me to continue, but my mind comes up blank for more than that. When he continues standing there, still and silent, I think back to what else could have set him off. "The slap..." I mutter as he places his fingers under my chins to lift my eyes to his.

"As much as I understand why you did it, I will not allow it again. Understand?"

"Yes."

"Now, since you couldn't keep your hands to yourself, you are going to stay right there and watch..." His fingers deftly undo his belt and zipper, revealing that he isn't wearing anything underneath and making my mouth water at the thought of tasting him. My fingers clench at my sides, itching to feel his skin against mine, but I know I need to stay still.

He pulls out his cock, fisting it in his hand, and my breathing picks up. Almost unconsciously, I start to lean forward.

"Not an inch, Little Bug." I pull back and rest my ass on my feet, hoping this punishment will be over soon, because I don't know how much more of this I can take.

"You like watching me jerk off? You like watching as I touch something you can't?" I lick my lips and close my eyes as his groans fill the room. "Eyes on me, Jade," he commands as arousal shoots to my core.

I watch as his fingers wrap around his tip, his eyes closing and his breathing becoming ragged the faster he moves. Just as I'm about to say screw it and beg once more for him to let me touch him, he stops.

"Are you ready to apologize, Little Bug?" His fingers leave his cock, caressing the side of my face instead as our eyes meet.

"Yes. I'm sorry for breaking the rules, and I'm sorry for slapping you..." He takes a deep breath, his thumb tracing my bottom lip.

"Open." His command is stern, though the strain in his neck tells me exactly how strung out he is.

I can't help the shudder that flows through my body, causing a chuckle to rumble in his chest. "How could I forget how much my woman loves being a bad little girl?" *Damn him and his words.* They travel over my skin like water and sink deep, leaving me wet and wanting. I suck his thumb into my mouth, moaning at the way his body shudders. Before he utters another word, I lose my remaining self-control and reach out to grasp his cock, my eyes drifting closed at the familiarity of his skin against mine.

"*Shit.* You have no idea how good it feels to have you like this again..." The words are hushed, and by the serene look on his face, I don't think he meant to say them out loud. Warmth fills my chest as I rise higher, my lips a breath away from the tip of his cock, waiting for the command I know will come. "Suck my cock, Little Bug... *Now.*" I release a breath, my entire body quaking with relief as my lips wrap around his shaft. I love the exhale that leaves him.

I don't wait for any further instruction as the memory of what he loves rushes back to the forefront of my mind. I wrap one hand around his girth, the other hand cupping his balls, squeezing lightly as his head falls forward, one hand shooting out to rest against the door behind me, the other palming the back of my head.

"Just like that...*shit*," he grits out, his hips jutting forward, causing his cock to penetrate my throat, making me gag a little. The groan he releases at the sound causes arousal to shoot straight to my core, my knees locking together as I squirm under his gaze. My eyes lift, meeting his hooded gaze as his fingers curl into the loose strands of my hair. I can't hold myself back any longer. My hand releases his balls and falls between my legs, attempting to relieve the pressure that builds every time his fingers pull me closer.

The shudder that rushes through me as my fingers dip past my waistband to find my pussy wet and wanting causes Gage to still. "What do you think you're doing, Jade?" he mutters, pulling me up off my knees as he crowds me against the door. "You know that your pleasure is mine and mine alone." I *do* know this. I knew it the second my fingers touched my sex. But what I *really* wanted was this, right here. Him leaning close, his lips trailing up the side of my neck, causing my knees to buckle under the weight of my desire. It's worth any possible future punishment.

"You know that your pussy is mine to please. But it's been so long, it's probably forgotten the way I can make it come so good...right?" My head falls back, hitting the wall behind me as my eyes close at just the thought of what's about to happen. I've dreamt about this, wished for it, and even though I knew it was unhealthy, I've gotten myself off to this exact scenario, knowing it's the only way I can feel something.

Anything.

"Keep those talented fingers wrapped around me, little bug, and I'll make you feel better." My eyes open, locking on his as he pushes me against the wall harder, one hand grabbing the back of my head as his lips whisper across mine. I open my mouth, almost ready to beg him to touch me, when his lips seal to mine, causing every thought to leave my brain.

The kiss is rough, mind-numbing, and all-consuming. Everything about Gage surrounds me—the way his breath feels tangling with mine, the way he fists the loose strands of my hair, and definitely the way his body molds to mine as his fingers delve beneath the waistband of my pajamas, hovering over my wet folds. The second the pads of his fingers touch my sensitive skin, my entire body dissolves in pleasure, causing my head to lean back once more, and my hands to fall to my sides. It's been so long since I've felt this kind of euphoria. This intense, heightened, eager kind of revelry that leaves every limb of my body weak.

Just as my body starts to buck against his touch, his fingers leave my heat and grasp my hips to push me away from his body.

"What did I tell you, little bug?" His fingers push past my waistband once more, this time with force. Before my brain has time to catch up, he plunges two fingers into my pussy, causing an instant orgasm that consumes my entire being. "*That's it.* I knew I could still make you come in an instant. You never could resist my touch. You're mine. You've always been mine...only *mine.*"

Those words are like a cold bucket of ice water dumped over my head. Every sensation that just consumed me vanishes into thin air as I shake my head, pulling his hand out of my pants and pushing him with everything I have.

And, of course, he doesn't budge.

Fucking muscles.

"What the hell, Gage?" I yell, shoving him harder with every ounce of strength I have left, but he doesn't move an inch.

"Jade," he whispers, his eyes pleading with mine as I try to decipher the pain I see in their depths. His fingers continue digging into my hip as my veneer starts to crumble. Everything I've felt over the past six years comes rushing back to the surface, and before I can think better of it, I smack him on the chest.

"Why?" I scream, feeling my body start to shake, tears forming behind my closed eyes. A feeling of obliterating anger rises up and rushes through me. "Why did you leave me alone? Why did you break me, only to come back here and shatter me all over again after I collected all the pieces you left scattered on the floor?" He shakes his head, but I don't let him speak as my breath continues coming in pants, leaving me almost lightheaded as I try to form the words I know he needs to hear.

"I loved you. I loved you more than I ever thought possible. And you just left like I meant nothing."

"That's a lie, and you know it."

"Do I? How would I know that, Gage? How would I know how you felt? Just when things got hard, when I asked for something from you that didn't involve sex, you bailed." He starts to shake his head again as a I push past him, wanting nothing more than to be away from his touch. Because I know the more he touches me, the quicker I'll cave.

"Parker is my best friend," he states, pulling up his pants and looking at me as if that explains everything.

"And he's my fucking *brother.* But you know what? I loved you enough to sacrifice the possibility that he'd hate me, just for the chance at happiness. But you were too much of a coward to do the same." I expect something more than the silence that surrounds me when I finish. I expect him to fight for me, for us, the way I always dreamed he would. The way I wished he would've done all those years ago.

"And just like last time, you still can't do it, can you?" His eyes narrow, asking the question his mouth can't. "You can't stand there and tell me you want more, can you? I know you loved me back then. I felt it every time you touched me. For fuck's sake, Gage, the way you touched me tonight tells me those feelings are still there. But so is your hesitance. If you can't tell Parker about us, then you can leave." I point toward the door, feeling the tears start to form once again as the man I've tried to keep from loving turns and walks toward the closed front door.

"Just so you know, I did love you. Still do." I can't help the laugh that escapes my throat.

"Just not enough." And with that, he opens the door and leaves me crumbling to the living room floor for the second time. Making me wonder what I did in this life to deserve the man I love causing me so much pain.

CHAPTER 8

Gage

"What is wrong with you, man? You've been off since you got here," Parker says as he sits on the couch and turns on some music from his phone. It's been three days since I left Jade's apartment, and I haven't done much but sit and stew over why I walked away and how I could leave her there like that. The look on her face when I left still haunts me, and I hate myself for the fact that I didn't tell her I'd do anything to make her happy. So, when Parker called and asked if I was up for a party, the answer was a resounding no. But I couldn't explain why, so I just decided to suck it up and head over to his place.

That was a big mistake.

Pictures of Jade are everywhere I look, and every

time I glance over at my best friend, I see his sister staring back at me, begging me to love her enough to fight for what we both want.

"Gage, three o'clock," Parker mumbles, nudging me with his elbow as he starts kissing the neck of some girl that sat on his lap. "She's been checking you out since you got here." I look to my right and see a gorgeous girl with bright red hair, blue eyes, and legs for days. Before I can think better of it, I get out of my chair, hearing Parker mutter something about getting laid behind me, and head toward the girl who clearly wants more than just a conversation.

"Hey there, handsome." Her fingers graze the exposed skin of my chest that peeks out from the collar of my shirt. "I haven't seen you around here before..." Her words are breathy, wistful, and a bit desperate, and repulsion starts in the pit of my stomach and rolls through my body with every pass of her fingers against my skin. But I try to push that away, shove it all down and hope for something, anything, to help me get the image of Jade out of the recesses of my mind.

Her lips lightly brush the column of my neck, and as I close my eyes, I briefly feel desire start to build. I almost feel a sense of normalcy rise, something I haven't felt since starting with Jade six years ago.

"You like that?" Red whispers in my ear as her

fingers find my cock. For a split second, I wonder if I should just fuck her. Do it and see if I can get over Jade once and for all. But the second her lips trail up my neck and land on mine, I push her away.

"Sorry, I can't," I croak, feeling my entire body back away from a woman any other man would kill to have against him. Yet here I am, comparing the way her fingers feel against my skin to the way Jade knows just the right pressure to use to cause both pleasure and pain. I'm comparing how Red smells like a meadow to how Jade smells like coconuts and fresh vanilla. And the way Jade's hair always seems to flutter against my skin the closer she gets to me, where this woman's does not.

"Are you serious right now?" she sneers, but I don't answer or wait to take in the earful I'm sure I'll hear if I stay. I just head toward the front door, ignoring Parker's voice asking where I'm going.

I need to fix this.

"Where is she?" I ask the second the roommate opens the door.

"And why would I tell you?" Her hands land on her hips as her head tips to the side, eyes narrowing the longer I stand in front of her. "She was crying. You have anything to do with that?" *Shit.* The cavernous hole in the pit of my stomach grows as the image of Jade crying forms in my head.

What have I done?

"Please, just tell me where she is," I beg, hoping Jade's roommate has a romantic side and sees what I'm trying to do. "I need to talk to her. I *have* to talk to her."

"She's at Temptation." The words have barely left her mouth before I'm thanking her and running down the stairs to my car. This is good. It's where it all started, so it's fitting it's where it will all come to a head.

It doesn't take me long to get to the club. I park down the street and jog up to the establishment. The closer I get to the front door, the more my nerves catch up to me. I hope to God that I'm not too late; that I haven't erased everything we created in one fell swoop.

"Gage, man, it's good to see you!" Nick says from the front door. I haven't been on shift with him, so I didn't get a chance to catch up yet. "I didn't know you were working tonight," he says.

I shake my head. "Not working tonight." He knows my history as he opens the door for me.

"It's nice to see you, man." For a split second, I see what all the girls rave about. The dark skin, bright smile, and a physique that makes even me envious. But he's been a good friend and someone I admire. Before I think better of it, I ask Nick for a favor. When his eyes bulge, and that knowing smirk crosses his lips, I know he'll help me out.

"Sure thing, man. I'll call upstairs and make the reservation."

Ignoring him, my mind is already on mission to find my woman so we can figure this shit out. I'm done playing games. If she wants me to talk to Parker, I will. If she wants me to write it in the sky in fireworks, I'll do that, too. I just need her in my life.

Just as I walk through the foyer, I stop dead in my tracks because the place is jam-packed, something I should have known since it's Friday night. But I curse, knowing it'll take me that much longer to find Jade. I scan the room quickly, seeing nothing but couples, demonstration, and aroused onlookers as I head toward the bar, hoping Sal can help me out.

"What can I get you, Gage?" he asks as I reach the bar. I shake my head and refuse the drink he offers to make.

"Have you seen Jade?" I ask. As his already pale skin gets lighter, the pit in my stomach grows. His gaze focuses on something behind me, so I turn. Once my eyes find the scene in question, everything around me stops. The music pumping out of the speakers turns into a dull roar as my mouth goes dry, my eyes focusing in on Jade as she dances with a guy I've seen around before. That's not what causes my stomach to drop, though. It's the fact that he has his lips on her skin, and his hand up her skirt. And from the look on her face, she loves it.

I'm too late.

CHAPTER 9

Jade

My eyes close as my hips shift and I hope to feel something, *anything* as the guy's hand drifts farther and farther past the hem of my dress, skimming the edge of my panties. My head drops back, and I grasp the back of his head so his lips can find purchase on the hollow of my neck. I pray to whoever is listening that I start to enjoy this. I need to get the image of Gage out of my head, and this is the only thing I could think of that might erase him from my memory.

But it's not working.

His hands feel wrong.

His grip is too timid, his lips too gentle, and he smells like Irish Spring soap, not sandalwood with a touch of vanilla.

It's all wrong. And when I open my eyes, I catch sight of someone that looks a lot like Gage. For a split second, I believe he's real, the way his eyes bore into me, and the way his fists clench at his sides. But especially the way his lips curve into a frown as my hips continue pulsing against the man behind me. Just as I close my eyes once more, hoping to get Gage's image out of my head, a voice says against the shell of my ear, "You know better than this, little bug." I gasp, pulling away from the guy I've been distracting myself with for the last hour, and come face to face with the man of both my dreams and my nightmares.

"Back off, man. She's with me," the mystery guy snarls as Gage gives him his signature smirk that still causes my knees to weaken. I roll my eyes, hating the bravado coming off him. I start to walk away when someone holds me back.

"Where are you going? We're not done..." Mystery guy's eyes stare, pleading with mine as I shake my head.

"Nope. We're done. I'm done. With both of you." I start to walk away, but someone pulls me back. This time, I'm spun and land against the hard chest of the man I've tried to get out of my head for the last three days.

"I don't think so, little bug, we're far from done," he mutters as he takes my hand and leads me past the demonstration, past the dance floor, and by the bar where Sal gives me a knowing smile.

"Where are we going?" I ask, knowing he won't answer, not now. He leads me upstairs, and my heart starts to race because there is only one reason he would bring me upstairs. I stop dead in my tracks. "Gage, no. I can't go up there with you. I'm not ready. *We're* not ready for that." When we first came here all those years ago, I wanted to go up into those private rooms. I desired the experience, but Gage always told me you had to have complete trust in the other person to go into one of those rooms. You had to be committed to catering to their every desire, fantasy, and dark thought. For Gage, the room was a symbol of his devotion, and although that wasn't true for everyone, for him, it was a big deal. So, right now, standing on these stairs, watching as he spins around to look me in the face, I'm nearly as confused as I was the first time he brought me here.

"We can't go up there. *I* can't go up there." I stand firm when he leans over, staring me directly in the eye.

"I know you think I don't love you the way I should. I know you think I can't handle telling your brother about us. But you're wrong. I will do anything you want...I'll yell it from the rooftops if you want. I just want *you*." My breath comes in pants, and my ears start ringing as his words register. "I can't live without you, Jade. I can't function without you around me, and believe me, I've tried. I tried for six years, and I failed horribly. I know you want my declaration of love, I know you want more than those words, but right now, I need to go into this room and prove to you that what we have is real. That what we have can withstand anything that comes our way. Because right now, all I can think about is going in there and fucking you the way I need to fuck you before I go insane."

Six years. I waited six years to hear those words, and all I can do is close my eyes as he takes my hand in his and leads me into the private room that holds everything I have ever wanted.

The second the door closes, the air around us changes, becoming charged with something I can't describe. Desperation? Anticipation? All I know is that the look in his eyes causes my breath to catch as he takes off his leather jacket and lifts his arms above his head, pulling his shirt off. For the first time, I get a full look at the man before me. He's like a sculpture, created from stone to test every ounce of my self-control. The tattoos are something to write home about as my eyes take in the colors and designs that take up his entire chest, running down his arms and past his knuckles. Skulls, roses, and sunsets, all hidden behind dark, faded clouds, angel wings, and tribal markings. It's a work of art, and my hand itches to touch them. But as I lift my hand, he grabs my wrist, grasping it with enough force to cause a flicker of pain that sends arousal straight to my core.

"Strip. Now," he demands, and a whimper escapes as my eyes close of their own volition. This is what I've always wanted. Him, surrounding me, causing my body to react in a way it doesn't with anyone else. "I will not ask you again, little bug." I bow my head, my fingers grasping the zipper pull on the side of my dress, slowly lowering it until the top falls off my shoulders. Before the garment has a chance to fall to the floor, Gage is in front of me, his fingers grasping the loose fabric as his lips trail down the column of my neck.

"Jesus..." I mutter involuntarily, and by the chuckle that vibrates against my skin, Gage seems pretty proud of himself. "Gage..." I whimper, my hands trailing up the sides of his torso, fingers tracing the tattoos as I go.

"Jade..." My name coming off his lips sends shivers throughout my entire body, and I know if he doesn't make a move soon, I'll combust right here. Just as I open my mouth to beg, even knowing the consequences, he spins me around, my dress falling to the floor. My eyes land on a four-poster bed sitting against the far wall. I don't notice the sheer canopy curtains, or the fact that the bedspread looks like it likely costs more than a month's rent. What I do focus on are the restraints that hang from each post. What I comprehend is the silk fabric that Gage now trails against my exposed skin.

"You have no idea how gorgeous you look right now." His light kiss on my shoulder catches me off guard as his fingers trace patterns on my stomach, causing every muscle in my body to contract. "Do you know what I've been dreaming about since we stepped foot in this place six years ago?" I shake my head, knowing he won't wait for an answer. "You, tied to this bed, at my complete mercy." His breath cascades over the shell of my ear, and I can't control the sound that leaves my body at the image he just placed in my head. "But do you know the best part?" he asks, nipping my sensitive skin. "You won't be able to see a thing..." He trails off as the silk fabric brushes against my skin once more.

"I won't?" I whimper, my voice shaking with desire as Gage pulls the silk away and carefully places it over my eyes.

"I don't want you to see what I'm about to do to

you. All I want you to do is feel, listen, and embrace the sensations, okay?"

"Yes," I whisper as he softly covers my eyes, tying the blindfold behind my head and leading me across the room. I know he's taking me toward the bed, but when I'm spun once more, my arms are lifted above my head, and my hands secured to the ties on the post, my breath starts to come in pants. I know what's coming, but we've never done anything like this before. I've never been completely at his mercy. I've always been able to escape.

Gage must sense my panic because his lips kiss the crook of my neck softly, and his hands come up to frame my face as he pulls down the blindfold. When my eyes adjust and meet his, all the panic in me recedes.

"You okay with this?"

"Yes," I whisper, loving that he can still show me this softer side of him, even when he's like this.

"You remember your safe word?" he asks, taking my face in the palms of his hands so our eyes lock.

"Kiwi." His smirk tells me he remembers when I picked it, knowing I hate the fruit and how fuzzy it is.

"Good girl," he whispers against my lips before he replaces the blindfold, and darkness surrounds me once again. Gage takes a second to check the ties, making sure they aren't too tight before he murmurs,

"I've been dreaming about this for years, and you are so much better than any fantasy I could ever conjure up." With that, his hands dig into the fabric of my panties, ripping them from my body before his fingers find my heat.

I shudder at the sensation, knowing that everything will change after tonight.

CHAPTER 10

Gage

J*esus,* she looks incredible standing against the bedpost, arms tied above her head, mouth open in ecstasy as my fingers circle her folds. Everything I've dreamed about doing to her in this room comes crashing into my subconscious, but I push them all away. Instead, I focus on the woman in front of me and the way her breath hitches every time the pads of my fingers hit her clit.

"Gage..." She moans, and I smirk, loving the look of complete submission on her face. I never thought I'd be the kind of man who loved giving pleasure instead of receiving it—and I certainly didn't think that way in college. But with Jade? Everything changed. The way she submits to me when we're like this yet gives me hell out in the real world gets me off easier and better than any useless lay I've had. That realization was what knocked me on my ass and ultimately brought me here, trying my best to show her that I'm all in. Forever.

"You know better than to beg, little bug..." I mutter against her ear, loving the way her body shudders at the thought of what I'm about to do to her. "*Fuck*," I curse as my fingers find that her folds are soaked. The second they plunge into her, I melt. "I forgot how wet you get with me." She doesn't say a word, just grips the ropes above her head and holds on for dear life as I slowly kiss down the column of her throat and move past her collarbone, paying particular attention to each of her breasts before trailing across her navel to stop at the apex of her thighs.

I groan at the smell of her arousal, and I know the second I get my mouth on her, I won't be able to stop. I won't be able to control the way my body reacts.

"Please..." she mutters, my fingers stopping as she cries out in frustration, knowing the mistake she made. "I'm sorry, please don't stop. Gage..." I can't help the smirk that comes from her trying to walk back the begging and then begging again.

"You're lucky I'm dying to taste you, or I'd make you wait," I say, right before my lips surround her clit, sucking her, biting her, and licking her until she's writhing beneath my touch.

"*Gage! Gage, Gage, Gage...*" She screams, causing my dick to harden even more as my hand lowers, trying to alleviate some of the pressure. The louder she calls my name, the harder it is to hold off fucking her like I've dreamed about doing since the day I left.

"I need you to come for me, little bug. I need to feel you come all over my fingers so I can fuck you. Come for me, Jade." On that command, she detonates, and it's the most beautiful thing I have ever seen. A flush of pink crosses her chest, traveling past her breasts and stopping at her navel. It's the last straw. I stand, stripping off my pants, and before I think better of it, I lift her off the floor, her legs automatically wrapping around my waist as my cock sinks deep into her heat.

"Shit..." I curse, feeling her warmth surrounding me as my entire body stills. I forgot how good she felt wrapped around me. I forgot what it felt like to feel her skin against mine. "Shit...condom." I mutter, silently cursing myself for forgetting, but before I start to pull out, she locks her legs around me and grins.

"Don't you dare move. I'm on the pill." I groan at the dominance of her statement, and although I thrive on control, seeing her like this is one hell of a turn on.

But those words are all I need to hear before I start to fuck her like our lives depend on it. My hands find her hips, then grip her thighs as I fuck her with everything I have.

"Shit, Gage...*yes*!" she screams as I pound into her. I love that she's at my mercy, but I need more. I stop, laughing at Jade's grunt of disapproval as I untie her hands, adoring when they fall to my shoulders as she wraps them around me. Before I think better of it, I toss the blindfold aside and seal my lips to hers, devouring her taste as my cock hardens even more. I slowly walk toward the side of the bed, gently lowering her onto the satin sheets before pulling my mouth from hers.

Her look of confusion sends a bolt of arousal right to my cock, because all I want to do at this moment is mark her, let her know that she's mine and mine alone. But what I actually do shocks us both. I lower my head and lightly kiss her soft lips, nipping, sucking, and groaning at the taste. My fingers trace her sides, stopping just below her breasts as her hips lift off the bed so she can grind against my cock, causing my head to fall forward and rest against her chest.

"Jade, *baby...*" I groan as she lifts her hips one more time. This time, my cock finds her opening, and I sink into her heat once more. How did I forget how good she feels? "Baby, you keep doing that, and I'll come," I mutter, loving the sassy smirk that crosses her face. I didn't plan on making love to her tonight. I wanted to recreate what we had before. But this? The moment when her eyes meet mine as she starts to fuck herself on my cock, her fingers lacing through my hair and pulling my lips back to hers, is so much more.

It's love.

"I love you," I say against her lips. Her hips stop, and her body stills. When I lean back to look into her eyes, I see confusion. "I love you, Jade," I repeat, knowing she doesn't believe me. "I know you might not believe me, but I do. This, right here?" I say, pointing between us. "This is me loving you. Not the dominance, not the fucking against the side of the bed, but this," I say again, sinking into her deeper and deeper as her eyes roll back in ecstasy.

"This is what I want. I want to hold you, watch you come..." Her eyes close as I start to sink into her slowly, feeling her walls constrict around my cock with every stroke. "I just want *you,* little bug. You are everything I ever wanted." I feel her pussy start to clamp down harder as her moans grow louder. I continue my slow assault, grinding against her until I know she's one stroke away from coming. "I love watching you like this, baby...you have no idea how gorgeous you look taking my cock deep inside. But I need to feel you come on my dick. Come for me, love." The new nickname slips out, and that's what sets her off. Her back arches, her fingers digging into my arms as a scream of pleasure explodes out of her. All I can do is watch, feeling the tingle in my spine rising with every stroke. Before long, I'm going over the edge with her, groaning into her neck, loving the feeling of her arms wrapped around me as we both come down from a high neither of us expected.

"I love you, too." And for the first time in years, I'm content.

CHAPTER 11
Jade

"Did you mean it?" I say into the dark as the flicker of the candles casts a yellow glow around the room. It took me at least ten minutes after the room stopped spinning to realize they surrounded us, and another ten minutes for reality to crash over me.

"What do you mean?" Gage asks as his fingers lightly graze my bare back as my head rests against his hard chest. We haven't said a word since I told him I loved him, and honestly, the silence is killing me.

"What you said when we were...?" I trail off, embarrassment overtaking every other emotion I thought to express in this moment. What am I supposed to say? *Did you mean to say you loved me, or were you just saying that to get laid*?

"Jade, baby." He chuckles against the crown of my head. His head dips slightly so he can gently kiss the top of my head, and I wonder for a second if I'm dreaming. I wished for this on so many nights. This kind of intimacy, contentment. But it never came, and I began to wonder if it ever would. "Of course, I meant it." His voice is hushed as he kisses my temple once more before I raise my head, resting my chin against my hand so I can look at his face.

"Really?" My voice must convey how uncertain I am, because the look in his eyes breaks my heart. Gage lifts me off his chest and sits up with his back against the headboard. Before I question what he's doing, he pulls me toward him, making it so my legs straddle either side of his hips as he takes my face in his hands.

"I am so sorry, Jade." I tilt my head in confusion, part of me trying not to overthink what he's about to say. But when he leans in and kisses me softly, I melt into him once more. "I'm sorry for ruining everything. For running when I should have stayed and fought for you. For us." I start to shake my head, but he stops me by pulling me closer. I tangle my fingers in his hair. "I regretted leaving the second I got on that plane and every day since. And I know I don't deserve your forgiveness. I know I don't deserve a happily ever after with you. But I'm hoping you'll let me try and prove my worth." His fingers dig into the curves of my hips as I rest my head against his.

"Gage, you have no idea how broken I was when you ran." A strangled sound comes from his throat, but I keep my forehead resting against his, my eyes closed because seeing him right now might steal the words I need to get out. "I was head over heels in love with you, had been for years. And I think you knew that." He dips his head as his hands travel up my back, grasping my naked skin to pull me even closer.

"Being with you was everything I wanted it to be and more. You introduced me to a side of myself I didn't know existed. I felt seen, loved, and wanted...more than I ever had. Then everything changed that night at the club." The tears I thought were long forgotten come roaring back, and before I have a chance to catch them, Gage's thumbs wipe them away.

"I need you to know that I didn't leave because you said you loved me." His eyes catch mine just as they're about to roll into the back of my head. "It's true. I knew I loved you that night. Hell, I knew I loved you weeks before that. But I was too chickenshit to do anything about it."

"Then what was it? Parker?" I ask, already knowing the answer before he agrees.

"Jade, he's my best friend. There's an unwritten

rule about going after your best friend's little sister, and I honestly didn't know how he'd react. I was afraid to lose him." I jerk back, my eyes narrowing as the words sink in, causing anger to rise to the surface.

"So, you were afraid to lose him but not me? That's not love, Gage, not even fucking close." I start to get off his lap, but his arms tighten around me, anchoring me in place.

"I was selfish back then. I thought I could get over you. I thought I was in love with the idea of you. But the second I got on that plane, the moment I realized the life I left behind, I knew I had made the biggest mistake of my life. I knew that if I had the chance, I'd make things right. I'd make sure you knew exactly how I felt."

"What about Parker? He still doesn't know..." I say, my fingers gently gliding over his chest as his breathing evens out.

"I know. We'll do whatever you want. If you want to wait, we wait. If you want to go see him right now, then we'll go. I don't care anymore. I love you. I love *you,* Jade, and I'm not letting anything come between us. Not this time." Before I have a chance to say anything, he takes my face in his hands once more and devours my lips.

This isn't like before. This is passion without

dominance, this is love without control, and I'm slowly becoming addicted to it. I grasp his neck, pulling him closer as I rise to my knees, feeling his cock harden.

"What are you doing, love?" I moan at the new nickname, taking one of my hands and grasping his hardened flesh, relishing the shiver that moves through him.

"I'm trying something new," I whisper against his lips, nipping and sucking as my hips circle his tip, gasping every time it hits my clit.

"I love you so much," he declares, his lips moving down the length of my neck until he finds that spot below my ear that causes every muscle in my body to contract. "I love you, Jade," he mutters just before his hands grasp both of my hips and he pulls me down onto his cock, causing a guttural moan to leave both of us.

"Yes..." I groan, my arms flinging around his shoulders as my hips start to move, pulling him deeper and deeper until both of us gasp as he hits my g-spot, causing a tidal wave of new pleasure to course through my body.

"Is that...?" I nod, not having the words as his lips attack mine once more, and we both relish the feeling of being this close, this intimate. Not long after, we're both grasping at skin and swallowing moans as we start flying over the edge into oblivion.

I can only hope that reality doesn't ruin what we just created.

CHAPTER 12
Gage

Two weeks ago, I didn't know if I would ever get back to a place where Jade and I could be happy. Now, here I am, sitting on her couch, watching TV with her head in my lap as I stroke the strands of her hair that fell out of her ponytail. As mundane as the scene is, it's what I always wanted, and I will do anything to protect it.

I lean down and kiss the crown of her head, whispering, "I love you" just as the front door opens, and Parker's eyes meet mine.

"Knock much?" I yell as Parker holds up his hand, walking toward us.

"What the hell?" he sneers just as Jade jumps out of my lap and scrambles to her feet. "Seriously, Gage? My sister!?" His voice carries across the room as I stand, calmly bringing Jade to my side as my hand clasps the side of her waist. Her eyes lift to mine, and I give her a reassuring look.

"It's okay, little bug." She starts shaking her head as the fear I know still surrounds her comes crashing to the surface. Her eyes fill with tears as she grabs my wrist, her expression begging me not to leave her. I give her a small smile as I cup the side of her face and softly kiss her lips. "I love you, Jade. That is not going to change, okay?" I hold her gaze until I see the words sink in. "I'm going to talk to him all right?" That fear comes roaring back, and I kiss her one more time. "Nothing will change this. Change us. I promise."

"I love you," she says, kissing me one more time before looking at her brother. "Do not be a dick, Parker," she says as Parker holds up his hands and then points at me.

"Don't blame me. I had to walk into this house and see my best friend groping my sister!"

"Don't be so dramatic. We were cuddling. Calm yourself," Jade mutters. Jesus, I really need to get them away from each other before they come to blows.

"Okay, stop! Both of you!" My voice raises, but I take Jade's hand in mine and lead her out to the back deck. I close the door behind us and turn her away from the glass so the only thing she can focus on is me.

"Gage…" she warns, but I just give her a smirk and shake my head.

"Jade, love. I need you to let me talk to him." I can see she's trying to hide her fear, the worry of me leaving again, so I caress the side of her face with my thumb. "I promise you that nothing he says will change the way I feel about you. Nothing he says will make me run," I say, giving her a reassuring look. "I'm gonna go back inside and see Parker. You want to stay out here?" She agrees, wrapping her arms around herself as a stiff breeze comes through. Without a thought, I take off the hoodie I'm wearing and place it over her head. I let out a chuckle as I take her in. The arms dangle past her knees, her hands nowhere to be seen, and the bottom of the sweatshirt is so long on her it could be a dress.

"What?" she says, looking down at herself, holding her arms out to the sides as I burst out laughing. "I think it's a perfect fit, don't you?" I shake my head and wonder why I ever thought that being away from her was a good idea. How could I have looked at this magnificent woman and wondered for even a second if she was worth it? She is more than worth it.

"You look perfect," I admit, loving the way her eyes soften as she comes toward me. I envelop her in my arms. "I'll be back soon, okay?" She nods against my chest as I place a soft kiss on her temple.

. . .

"Don't even start," I say, walking back into the house as Parker comes toward me. "Your sister doesn't need to hear you yelling, so let's go out front." I gesture to the front door as he agrees, keeping an eye on Jade as I walk past. The second we get outside and I shut the door, he's on me.

"My sister, Gage? Seriously?" I take a deep breath and lean against the railing as he props himself against the windowsill opposite me.

"I didn't plan for this, man," I admit as he shakes his head and crosses his arms across his chest.

"When...how? Why...?" he starts, but I just laugh and motion for him to stop.

"It started six years ago..." I pause as his eyes bulge like I knew they would. And as I tell him the entire story from us crashing together, me leaving, and then finding each other again, he starts to understand.

"So, you're telling me that you joined the military to avoid telling me you were in love with my sister?" When I say nothing, he simply grins and shakes his head. "Dude, that's a bit extreme, don't you think?" I shrug because, at the time, I thought it was the right thing to do.

"What would you have done if I had come to you and told you I was in love with Jade?"

"Made you break it off." I give him the *I told you so* look, because that's exactly what I thought he'd say. "But I still deserved to know."

"I know, and I regretted leaving every day. But I had to get my shit together. Your sister is..." I stop, trying to think up the words to describe what she means to me. "Jade was inevitable. From the moment I saw her six years ago, I knew she was it. And it scared me. It scared me because I knew I could lose not only you but also her. That's why I left. I didn't want to pull you two apart any more than I already had." He quirks an eyebrow as I explain that she stopped seeing him as much because she was afraid he'd figure out that she and I were together.

"You really love her?" His eyes bore into mine, and for a second, I wonder if he'll beat the shit out of me if I agree.

"Yes." He sucks in a deep breath and takes the few steps until he's right in front of me. "Then I guess I have no choice but to accept it. But if you so much as breathe the wrong way around her, I will end you." I chuckle, sticking my hand out to take his.

"I swear on my life that I won't do anything to hurt Jade. Nothing." He nods and shakes, looking through the front window, which has a view of the back deck. “I think you two need to talk,” I say, looking in her direction.

“Yeah, I know,” he says, clasping my shoulder as he heads inside. I take one last look at Jade through the window before I sit down on the front stair and wait, knowing I have all the time in the world.

CHAPTER 13
Jade

"You look like you're drowning in that," Parker says as he comes through the sliding doors and sits in the chair next to me.

"Yeah, I know." I chuckle, holding out my arms so he can see just how big the sweatshirt is on me. I close my eyes and bring the fabric to my nose, smelling Gage and relaxing instantly. I don't know what they talked about; I don't know what Parker is thinking. All I know is that I will do everything in my power to keep Gage in my life, and that includes defying my brother.

"So, you love him, huh?" We're silent for a second before I blush, hearing him let out a breath as he leans back against the chair. "You know, when you were a kid, I always thought I'd be able to protect you from guys like Gage." I go to say something, but he stops me.

"Gage was always a player, ever since he grew four inches in ninth grade and started working out regularly. The girls were always all over him, and I could tell you were one of them." My eyes bulge, not realizing that he knew about my secret crush. "You were terrible at hiding it, but I thought once we went away to college, you'd get over it. I guess in a way, you did."

"Parker, what I felt for Gage in high school and what I feel for him now are not the same thing. Not even close."

"I know that. I also know that Gage is a different person now than he was back then. The Gage I knew was always with a different girl and was proud of it. But then, six years ago, he changed." My intake of breath must be a signal that I know what he's talking about because he gives me a small grin. "I didn't realize it then, but he did. He wasn't asking to go to clubs anymore, he wasn't flaunting a girl on his arm every chance he got. To be honest, I never saw him with anyone during that time And I know now that's because he was with you."

"Parker, we didn't mean to keep it from you..." He

laughs, looking my way as he takes my sweatshirt-covered hand in his.

"Yes, you did. But it's okay. I know why you did it." We sit there for a few minutes in silence before he speaks again. "Those few months I knew you were seeing someone, I could see the changes in you, even though you kept your distance." Guilt floods me as our eyes meet, and he gives me a sad look.

"It's okay, Jade. I get it now. I just wanted you to know that I noticed, and I could tell that whoever he was, he meant a lot to you." I take a deep breath and thank God that he gave me Parker as a big brother. "He told me he loves you...do you love him?"

I tilt my head to the side so our eyes meet before I say, "With everything in me. Parker, I've loved him for what seems like my entire adult life. When he left, when I asked him to tell you everything and he wouldn't, I was broken." He squeezes my hand, letting me know that Gage told him. "Being without him is harder than I ever thought possible. So, I need you to be okay with this. I need you to tell me it's okay to love him because I don't want to lose you. I told Gage that we could survive anything, and I thought that included the idea of you not being okay with this, but sitting here with you, talking to you about him, I need you to be okay with this so we can go back to the way it was. I miss spending time with you..." The tears start to fall as he pulls me off my chair and onto his lap. When his arms encircle me, I crumble, every emotion I've been holding onto for the past six years pouring out as my brother brushes the side of my head.

"You don't have to worry about me, okay? Do I love the idea of my best friend being with my baby sister? Not really." I tense against his chest as he continues. "But your happiness is more important than me being comfortable. I can learn to deal with your relationship. I can't deal with you being heart-broken and hating me for tearing you two apart." I start to cry harder, a feeling of utter relief washing over my entire body. "He loves you more than I have ever seen him love anything in his life. But you come to me if he fucks up. I'll kick his ass." We both laugh as I stay on his lap, loving being close to him again, missing the way he makes me feel safe and protected.

Before long, another set of arms surrounds me as I'm lifted against Gage's chest. I'm half asleep as I hear Gage and Parker saying goodbye to each other, and as if by magic, I feel the coolness of Gage's sheets against my bare legs.

"Sleep, love. We'll talk in the morning." I grin into his pillow, loving that his smell surrounds me.

"Love you," I say as he kisses the side of my neck.

"Forever," he whispers, curling up behind me, pulling me closer to his chest, enveloping me in his arms.

CHAPTER 14
Gage

I'm in the middle of cooking breakfast when I hear a yawn behind me. When I turn, I stop dead in my tracks. Jade is standing in my kitchen wearing nothing but one of my t-shirts, and I have to actively stop my jaw from dropping to the floor.

"What?" she asks, looking behind her as if she doesn't know how gorgeous she looks right now. I shake my head and turn back to the stove, trying to concentrate on the bacon and eggs cooking rather than thinking of all the ways I could ravish her against the kitchen wall.

"You don't like me in your shirt?" she teases, coming up behind me and kissing the middle of my back. I groan, trying to calm my dick, which is now standing at attention. Sleeping next to her was something I never thought I wanted, but feeling her wrapped around me, feeling her breath across my chest is like a drug. And I want more.

"Love, you know the shirt looks perfect on you. But the more I look at you, the more I want to see you out of it." I can feel her laugh as she wraps her arms around my middle, her fingers trailing dangerously close to my arousal. "Jade..." I warn, but she continues until I spin around and face her.

"It looks like you have something besides breakfast on your mind." We both look down as Jade bites her bottom lip, sending another bolt of arousal straight to my cock. Before she can get her hands on me, I turn away and plate our breakfast, taking it to the island and motioning for her to sit.

"You're no fun." I laugh as I take a bite, staring at her face as she eats.

"Sorry, but I think we need to talk about what happened yesterday." Her eyes meet mine, and I take her hand to reassure her that nothing I'm about to say will change the way I feel about her, but she seems unfazed.

"What is there to talk about?" She avoids my gaze as she takes her hand away and starts eating again.

"I want to make sure you're okay with everything.

With Parker knowing everything, and what that means for us." Her eyes meet mine again, and this time I see determination there.

"Parker has nothing to do with us," she says, our eyes locking. "Besides, he's okay with everything, so it's not even a blip on my radar right now."

"Fair enough. But I think since Parker knows about us, *we* should talk about us." Her eyes narrow in confusion. "I want you to know that I'm in this for the long haul. I want you to know that I'm not going anywhere."

"I know," she says, taking her last bite of egg and acting as if what I said isn't a big deal.

"You know..." I repeat before her eyes meet mine once more.

"Gage, I've known you almost my entire life. I've loved you for that same amount of time. Now that Parker knows about us, nothing's standing in our way. For the first time in a long time, I feel happy. Pure, unfiltered happiness that I didn't know was possible until you stepped back into my life. So, if you're on the same page, then what's the problem?" I don't say anything for a long time, just stare at her as she picks up our dishes, walks around the island, and places them in the sink.

She's perfect.

That's all I can think about as I stalk toward her, spin her around, and seal my lips to hers, groaning at her taste as she jumps into my arms and wraps her legs around my waist. The kiss starts off sweet but quickly grows into something more.

"I love you," I say against her lips as I walk us up the stairs, pushing her against the wall just outside my bedroom, groaning at the feeling of her heat grinding against my cock.

"I know," she says, nipping at my ear as my lips trail down her neck, causing her head to hit the wall in ecstasy. "But if you don't get us into that bed soon, I can promise I will never, ever say it back again." I burst out laughing, kissing her lips hard as I take us into my bedroom, making sure she never has a reason not to say that she loves me.

Epilogue

GAGE

"So, you're really doing this?" Parker asks as I take back the ring and place it into my pocket where it's been for the last few months. I knew the night we told Parker that I wanted to spend the rest of my life with Jade, but I also knew she needed time. And to be honest, I was happy to be along for the ride.

"Yeah, I just hope it goes according to plan," I admit, knowing Parker has no idea how I'm doing it. If I told him, I would have to explain Club Delirium and why it's special to Jade and me. And I'm honestly not ready for him to know that side of our relationship.

"Well, if she says no, I'll have a case of beer in the fridge for you." He's joking, but the idea of Jade saying anything but yes causes my chest to constrict. "Don't worry, man. My sister loves you, and if the last two years aren't proof enough, I don't know what else to tell you." I smirk, thinking back on the last two years and wondering why I ever thought my life would be better without her in it. If anything, I'm a better man now than I was before I admitted my feelings for her. She's my light, my beacon. My everything.

It took a while for Parker to get used to the idea of his little sister being in a relationship with his best friend, but in the end, it worked out really well. We go to his place every other weekend for dinner, and he helped us move into our house a few months ago, making it known that anything going into the master bedroom would be our responsibility, and that he refused to step foot in any place I would defile his sister. He has no idea that what happens in that room is nothing compared to what happens at the club. We go there at least once a month because my girl can't go that long without being tied up or being the exhibitionist I love so much—which is why I hope my plan for tonight works.

I look at my watch and realize I have to pick her up at work in half an hour, so I say goodbye to Parker and text Nick to make sure everything is set up. When I get a response telling me that everything's good, I take a deep breath and pray to God that she says yes.

"What are we doing here?" Jade asks as we stand outside Club Delirium. I don't say a word as I take her hand, leading her past Nick, who gives me a wink. The second we step onto the stairs, I hear her laugh behind me. "You know, if you wanted a kink night, you could have just asked." I chuckle, taking her hand and bringing it to my lips for a soft kiss.

"Little bug, you know I don't need your permission for that." I give her a wink as I lead the way to the room that started it all. The second we step in, and I shut the door, she gasps.

"Gage..." Her eyes scan the room that is once again filled with candles, but this time instead of rushing her, I take my time. I stand behind her, lightly brushing her skin with my fingers, causing her head to fall back against my shoulder.

"Still so responsive." I sigh as I pull up the fabric of her shirt, revealing her porcelain skin, inch by inch. "You have no idea how many times I've dreamt about you in this room...on your knees, taking everything I give you..." The words cause her to shudder as I lift her arms above her head, discarding her shirt on the floor and revealing the white lace bra that covers her breasts. "Take off your pants, love. *Now*." She does it in record time as I look to my right and see the blindfold I asked Nick to deliver. Once in my hands, I place the silk over her eyes, loving the sound of her breath catching in her throat.

Once tied, I lead Jade toward the bed, lifting her hands above her head and tying them gently to the post, making sure she can easily get out if she wants.

"You remember your safe word, little bug?" I ask, loving the pink flush crawling up her skin.

"Yes."

"Good," I murmur against her flesh as I kiss down her chest, sucking hard on her nipples through the fabric of her bra before lowering to my knees, making sure to take out the ring as I go. "You know I love you, right?" I ask as her head dips, my lips trailing across her hips. "You know I would do anything to make you happy." She beams as I drag the ring across her skin. She jumps at the unfamiliar feeling, and her head tilts as she tries to figure out what it is.

"I've been thinking about this night for a long time. This room where I showed you how much I loved you will be the room where I show you that I will continue to love you for the rest of my life."

"What—?" she starts as I stand, my fingers trailing against her side as I lean in, kissing her neck right before stopping at the shell of her ear.

"I want to spend the rest of my life with you, Jade. I want to have children with you, I want it all, love. I want all of you." Tears spill out from under the blindfold, and I kiss them away softly. "So, I guess there's only one question I need to ask. But before I do, I need to see your eyes," I say, taking off the blindfold and tossing it aside. When her gaze meets mine, her focus drifts to the ring I'm holding in front of her, and the tears flow freely as a smile the likes of which I have never seen before crosses her face.

"Jade, love, little bug...Will you marry me?" She closes her eyes, her hands fighting against the restraints as my hand cups the side of her face, bringing her forehead to mine. "Please, baby, make me the happiest man on the face of the Earth and say you'll be mine forever. Please..."

"I thought you would never ask..." She cries as our eyes meet, and I see utter devotion staring back at me.

"Is that a yes?" I ask, needing to hear the words.

"Yes." She nods. "Yes, I will marry you. I will marry you over and over if you ask. I love you so much."

"Now, to celebrate." I breathe onto her neck as I release her hands and then throw her onto the mattress. "Wonder how long it will take for you to get pregnant..." I tease as her eyes widen, a small smile crossing her lips.

"I guess we'll have to find out," she says as she pulls me close, taking the ring from my fingers and placing it on hers. And, just like that, everything feels exactly the way it's supposed to. I kiss her hard, tearing off the rest of her clothes. When she wraps her arms around my neck, I know I'm where I'm supposed to be.

Jade is my home.

Bonus Story

Want to know what happened to Halley and Ian? Continue reading for their love story!

TEMPTING
A TEMPTING FATE NOVELLA
You
S.A. CLAYTON

CHAPTER 1

Halley

The second I walk through the front door of Hardy's, the swanky downtown bar, my heart sinks, and I take a breath. *I need to know the truth.* I need to know if those text messages were real, and if they were, I need to see them with my own eyes.

My eyes scan the room, trying to see if Brad is here, and when I don't see his telltale blond head anywhere in sight, I breathe a sigh of relief. *Maybe tonight won't be as bad as I think.* I take a tentative step toward the bar, and the first thing I notice is the bartender. Tall and slim, with a five o'clock shadow that accentuates his jaw. The closer I get, the more intrigued I become. His black hair is splattered with dark-blue dye, a contrast that highlights his bright-blue eyes, and when they connect with mine, I can't help the way my heart stutters.

"What can I get you?" he asks, his voice low, sending a sensation coursing through my body that I haven't felt in months. My eyes take in everything about this man—the black T-shirt monogrammed with the bar's name on his chest, the silver chain around his neck, and the spacers in his ears. All of these things make me question why he's working in a place like Hardy's. The clientele here are primarily businessmen who come in wearing suits and ties, drink brandy neat, and pay with a black card. But the longer my eyes scan this man from head to toe, the more intrigued I become. "Miss?" he questions, snapping my eyes to his as he graces me with a smile that tells me just how obvious I was in checking him out. "Do you want a drink?" he asks once more, this time leaning on the bar as I take a seat at one of the empty barstools.

"Sorry," I mutter, my cheeks flaming red. My fair skin hides nothing as he winks and stands back to his full height. That's when the front door opens, and my eyes connect with the couple entering the bar. The second I see that blond hair come into view, every fear, every horrible thought I've had over the past few hours comes rushing to the surface.

There, in front of my eyes, is my boyfriend of three

years with his arm around his secretary, who looks stunning in her tight pencil skirt, white blouse, and pin-straight blonde hair tied up in a high ponytail. For a split second, I wonder if my eyes are deceiving me. Maybe he's just having a meeting with her after work? Then he smiles the smile that used to be reserved for me and leans down, kissing her on the lips as if it's the most natural thing in the world.

"Shit," I whisper as the tears begin, my hands shaking as I take out my phone and read over the messages I received not even three hours ago.

Unknown: *Your boyfriend isn't who you think he is. He's been seeing his secretary for months.*

Unknown: *Go to Hardy's at six tonight, and he will be there with her.*

Unknown: *I'm sorry.*

"Are you okay?" the bartender asks, those crystal-blue eyes full of concern. I shake my head, letting the tears fall because who the fuck cares at this point. I can't tell if the tears are from sadness or anger, but it doesn't matter right now. All I want to do is go over there and bitch-slap him so hard his mother feels how much of a douche canoe her son is. "That your boyfriend?" His voice is quiet, reserved, and when my eyes meet his, I see pity staring back at me.

"Ex-boyfriend now," I mutter, feeling the anger

start to bubble up inside me. Brad promised me forever, even though deep down, I knew he wasn't what I wanted. I wanted spice, I wanted lust, and I definitely wanted more than one orgasm every few weeks. But I stayed because he's what I thought I needed. Already in my late twenties, I wanted to get married, and everyone always said we made the perfect couple. I believed them.

"Did you know he would be here?" he questions, a brow lifted, and a concerned look plays behind those eyes that have quickly become my favorite part of this man. I nod, taking out my phone and showing him the text messages. "Wow. Well, I guess it's better to know now than waste more time."

"You could say that," I say, wiping away the stray tears that have fallen and are now staining my cheeks. "I just can't tell if I'm more angry or sad at this point. I mean, we've been together three years, and I thought it was going somewhere even though our sex life left a lot to be desired..." My eyes widen, and I slap my hand over my mouth because I can't believe I just said that.

"Well, then he doesn't deserve you." God, this is so embarrassing. I shake my head and place my face in the palm of my hands, wanting the floor to open up and swallow me whole. "Any man who can't satisfy his woman shouldn't have her in the first place." God, it just keeps getting worse.

"I can't believe I just told you that...you're a total stranger." He smiles, holding out his hand as if waiting for me to shake it. I tilt my head in question, and when he nods for me to take his hand, I smile, doing as he says.

"Hi, my name is Ian Walker. I own this bar and hate potato chips." His eyes are smiling, and I can't help but do the same.

"You hate potato chips? How is that even possible?" I chuckle, loving how he completely took me away from the moment with a single touch.

"Yes," he states matter-of-factly, as though he's not the most interesting person because of this fact. "Now you." He nods to me, waiting.

"I'm Halley Parker. I love potato chips, and hate Skittles."

"See? You don't need to be embarrassed because we're not strangers anymore." God, this man is healing the crater in my chest with every sweet thing that comes out of his mouth.

"Touché, Mr. Walker." He smiles, pulling out the rag tucked into his back pocket and wiping down the already clean bar in front of us.

"Are you going to go over there and confront him?" the bartender asks as my eyes dart over to where Brad is sitting. The woman seductively plays with his tie, leaning in and kissing his neck, causing me to gag subtly.

"I want to...I need to." I admit, taking a deep breath and trying to figure out what I'm going to say, but my mind comes up blank. I wish my best friend, Jade, was here because she would know exactly what to say and how to say it. Before I can dwell on any of it, a shot glass appears in front of me. My eyes lift only to meet the glimmering ones of Ian, who just smiles and pushes the glass toward me.

"If you're going to go over there, I think you need this." I blush, knowing he's right. "Just so you know, he's an idiot."

"How do you know that? You don't even know me."

"Well, for one, I know your name is Halley, and you love potato chips. Something I won't hold against you, by the way," I can't help the laughter that bubbles up in my chest. "But in this case, I don't need to know you to know he's an idiot." God, those eyes bore into mine, and that weight on my chest lifts just a little bit, making me wonder if meeting him tonight was fate.

Taking one last look at the shot glass, I down it in

one go even though I have no idea what's in it and cough as the vodka hits my throat. I'm grateful when Ian then places a glass of Coke in front of me, and I take a sip.

"God, it's been a long time since vodka and I have seen each other." Ian chuckles low in his throat as he takes the shot glass off the bar and places it in the sink behind him. "Well, here goes nothing..." I mutter. Spinning in my chair, I take a deep breath, knowing that after this moment, my life will never be the same.

CHAPTER 2
Ian

Halley walked into my bar not even twenty minutes ago, and already, I can feel the itch in my fingers to touch her, claim her, and be the man her boyfriend obviously isn't. I watch as she walks toward the poor bastard, her head held high, shoulders back, and I can't help but wish I knew what she was about to say.

I want to be the one to tell him what an idiot he is, how colossal his mistake is because stepping out on a woman like Halley? That's not conceivable to a man like myself. I knew she was my type the second she walked through the door. Her bright-red hair is anything but natural, yet it suits her all the same. I didn't know I could find her sleeve of tattoos any more attractive, but pairing that with the nose ring and her extremely unexpected shy demeanor, and I was hooked.

I take my eyes off Halley to serve a few of my regulars and restock some of the beers under the bar. When I come back behind the bar, I expect to see Halley's arms flailing and hear her voice carrying across the room, but instead, her shoulders are slumped, and her head is dipped toward her chin.

Fuck.

I eye Hank, my other bartender, and he gives me a knowing smile, nodding for me to go save her. So I hop over the bar, dismissing the bulging eyes of some of the patrons, and make my way toward Halley.

"Halley. Go home, and we'll talk," Hank demands. Her shoulders lift as if she's taking a deep breath, and before she can let it out, I reach out and take her hand, pulling her against me, my lips close to her ear.

"I got you. Give him hell." Her body sinks back against my chest, entwining our fingers and squeezing as her eyes meet mine. I nod, letting her know she can do this, and that's when my eyes lift to meet the idiot who decided he was better than the woman in front of me.

"Who the fuck are you?" Douchebag mutters, the disgust evident as he takes in my appearance—from the blue hair, spacers in my ears, and the tattoos that cover almost every inch of my torso and arms. I know I don't fit the mold his type believes should be allowed within the front doors. But he's in for a shock.

"I'm the owner of this bar, and I think it's time for you to leave." He rolls his eyes as they flick back and forth between Halley and me.

"You hypocrite. You're over here yelling at me for getting some on the side when you're doing the same fucking thing!" he yells. Halley flinches as my arm wraps around her middle, pulling her closer.

"I never cheated on you," Halley whispers, her eyes cast down, and I know as much as she wishes to yell and scream at this guy, that's not her style. So I decide to do it for her.

"Okay, that's it. You and the girl need to leave." My voice carries, and all of a sudden, a hush settles over the bar, and all eyes are on us. Halley begins shaking in my arms, and I know I need to get her out of this situation before it gets any worse, so I gently pull her behind me as I lean down on the table between us and level our gazes. "I am going to say this one more time before I call the cops. Okay? I need you and the lady to leave my bar...now." He huffs, taking the woman's hand as they stand and walk away. Just when I think the drama is over, he turns when he reaches the front door and catches Halley's eyes.

"Call me later, Hal. We'll talk and sort all of this out." He smirks. The fucker smirks, thinking that everything will be okay while he's standing in front of her with another girl in his arms.

"You know," Halley says from behind me, finally stepping out, her shoulders back and eyes angry, "a few months ago, I might have done just that. A few months ago, I might have tried to make it work, but you know what? I'm done. I'm done getting shot down by you, I'm done feeling like what I want doesn't matter, and I'm sick and tired of feeling less than because your ego can't take it." Fuck, yeah. My hands settle on her shoulders, lightly squeezing and loving the smile she gives when her eyes meet mine. I'm so proud of her at this moment.

"That would be your cue to leave," I say, pointing at the door. I wait until they're out of sight before spinning Halley on her heels and wrapping my arms around her, pulling her close. "God, that was awesome," I mutter into her hair, taking a deep breath and shuddering at the strawberry scent that hits me.

"Thank you for that. I was prepared to yell and scream, but when I got over there, that woman was looking at me with so much pity in her gaze... I just couldn't do it." I nod, taking her hand in mine, trying to ignore the spark that travels through me.

"Well, you did it, and I think that deserves a drink on the house." She smiles a genuine smile for the first time tonight, and I wink, settling her on her stool and making my way around the bar once more. "What can I get you?" Her eyes sparkle as her head tilts, her eyes locking with mine.

Yup, it's going to be hard to get this woman out of my head for the foreseeable future.

"An old-fashioned please." Fuck, but I love when women order something that doesn't come either slushed or with an umbrella or a cherry.

"A woman after my own heart," I whisper, placing a napkin down on the bar. "Now the question is, do you want it with bourbon or whiskey?" I ask, hoping she gets the joke, and when her eyes sparkle, I know the earlier scene has drifted into the recesses of her mind.

"Well, considering bourbon is a type of whiskey, it seems that question is null and void," she teases, and I swear I fall for her headfirst at this moment. She's perfect.

"Well done," I whisper, loving the way her eyes dilate at the praise. I file that piece of information in the back of my mind as I take a minute to make her drink. I place it in front of her, watching as she takes a sip. "Halley approved?" I ask, needing to hear her praise.

"Yes, very well done," she mutters before taking another sip. Before long, that drink is gone, and I'm working on making her another.

"Can I ask you something?" She nods, her eyes meeting mine as I take a deep breath, not knowing if she'll find this out of line. "Why were you with a guy like that?" I nod to the door so we both know who I'm talking about. "He obviously didn't deserve you." She smiles, shaking her head.

"He wasn't always so..." She trails off, trying to find an appropriate word.

"Douchey?"

She laughs, nodding. "Yes, that. But these past few months, I've been...pushing to do some things he wasn't interested in pursuing."

I tilt my head in confusion. "Is that a roundabout way of saying you're into some kinky shit, and he wasn't?" She blushes scarlet, and I have to take a breath to settle my cock down because that color on her fair skin is causing him to go into hyperdrive.

"Maybe?" she whispers. Downing the rest of her drink in one go, she gets up off her stool and picks up her purse. "I think that's my cue to go before I embarrass myself any more for one night." A sense of panic settles in the pit of my stomach, and before I can think better of it, my mouth opens, and words spill out.

"Can I take you home?" Her brow lifts, and when I hear the words repeated back in my brain, I cringe, knowing how they sound. "What I mean is, can I drive you home? I want to make sure you make it home safe." From the way her eyes narrow and the uncertainty spills from her gaze, I don't expect to ever see this woman again after tonight. But to my surprise, she nods, blushing once more before smiling, and at that moment, I know everything is about to change.

CHAPTER 3

Halley

You can cut the sexual tension with a knife as Ian drives me home. The cab of his truck is thick with all the emotions swirling around us, and for once in my life, I want to be the one to do something spontaneous. I want to take what I want when I want it. But that small voice in the back of my brain fills my head, and I remember that I'm an adult, someone with a full-time job, responsibilities, and a life to think about. That doesn't stop me from dreaming about what Ian's lips would feel like devouring mine or what those tattooed hands would feel like gliding up under my shirt.

"You okay over there?" I nod, pointing at my building. "You're quiet." I smile, knowing he's right but not having any words.

When Ian pulls over, I don't wait for him to shut off the engine. I bolt out of the truck, knowing that if I stay a second longer, I would admit how much I want to kiss him, and that would lead to a discussion I don't know if I'm ready for.

"Halley!" Ian yells, jogging around the front of his truck and grasping my wrist lightly, stopping me in my tracks. "What's wrong?" When I turn to lie and say it's nothing, I see the concern painting over those gorgeous eyes, and my shoulders sag.

"I don't want to say," I admit, hoping that's enough because the thought of admitting anything else causes hives to break out over my chest. I expect him to let go, walk away, and never see me again, but he doesn't. Instead, he laces my fingers with his and pulls me flush against his chest.

"You know what I think?" he whispers, his lips grazing the shell of my ear and causing goose bumps to spread across every inch of my body. I shake my head, my eyes falling closed as the lips I've spent the past few hours fantasizing about kiss their way down my neck. "I think that you've been thinking about kissing me for the past few hours, just like I've been thinking the same damn thing." My intake of breath shudders through my chest as I try to control my limbs. "And as much as I want to take you upstairs and show you just how much you've been tempting me, I know you've just broken up with your boyfriend, and I'm not that guy." My eyes snap open, locking with his.

"What?" Breathless, I try to come up with something more to say because I know he means to be the good guy here, but the more he says, the more I want to jump him right here.

"Halley, you walked into my bar as if I drew you myself. You are everything I want, yet tonight is not the night to do this. I can tell by the fear in your eyes that you're not ready for what I want, and that's okay. I'll bide my time." He winks and kisses me on the cheek before walking away, back toward his truck. It's then that the sense of panic sets in. The thought of never seeing him again settles under my skin and festers, and I know I can't let him walk away.

I've been locked in a relationship that left so much to be desired, and right now, I want to be the girl I always wanted to grow up to be. So I take one more deep breath before running after Ian, mirroring his move and grasping his wrist right before he reaches his truck. He spins, pushing me up against the side of his truck, and before I have time to explain what I was doing, his mouth is on mine.

I thought I knew what kissing was. I thought I knew what passion felt like once it wrapped itself around you, but this kiss from Ian blew everything I thought I knew out of the water and left me breathless.

"Thank God," he mutters against my lips before taking them once more, his fingers digging into my hips as he pulls me flush to his chest. "You have no idea how much I fought myself to keep from taking you in my truck on the way here. How much I wanted to taste these lips while you were sitting in front of me looking like you came right out of every fantasy I've ever had." I groan, my arms circling his neck as my leg lifts and hooks around his hip. His hand immediately grasps my thigh, lining his hard cock up to grind perfectly against my heat.

"Come upstairs with me," I say breathlessly, almost like a prayer, and when I'm met with silence, I open my eyes only to be met with hesitancy.

"I don't think that's a good idea," he warns, placing a soft kiss on my lips. I try to take it further, but he lets go of my leg before taking a step back. "Don't get the wrong idea here, babe. I want you so bad that my dick is literally screaming at me right now. But can you honestly say you're ready for all of that tonight?" My hesitancy is enough for both of us, and my shoulders sag in defeat.

"I'm sorry." Humiliation settles deep within my

bones, and before I can wallow in it, Ian is there, wrapping his arms around my shoulders.

"Halley, I like you, and I want to see where this goes, but I need you to be sure." God, it's like he was drawn just for me.

"What if I can't give you more than this?" I question, nerves plaguing my stomach as I search his eyes for a clue as to how he's feeling. "What if I can't do the relationship thing?"

"So you want to be friends with benefits?" he teases, and I smile, lowering my head to his chest as my fingers grasp the sides of his shirt.

"To be fair, we aren't even really friends." He gasps, his hand resting over his heart as if I've just insulted him. But his full-on smile gives his true feelings away, and I laugh.

Ian locks eyes with mine before lowering his lips in a sweet kiss that I know will linger for hours after he leaves. "I can handle just the benefits...for now." He winks and makes his way to the driver's side of the truck. "Come to the bar when you're sure this is what you want. I'll be there every night this week." I nod, watching as he drives away.

CHAPTER 4
Halley

"Are you sure getting with someone right after a breakup is a good idea?" It's been a few days since the night with Ian, and I haven't been able to get him out of my head. So naturally, I tell Jade, my best friend, that we need to do lunch because I need to talk it out.

"I know it seems fast." She gives me that *no shit* look, and I laugh. "But he makes me feel things I have never felt before in my life. Jade, that kiss was..." My eyes drift off, and I try to think of a way to describe it. "Colossal." Yet even that word doesn't seem adequate.

"I still think it's too soon."

I roll my eyes. "Prude," I joke, seeing a flicker of something behind her eyes, but before I can question it, our server arrives to take our order.

"Halley, you just broke it off with Brad after you've been with him for over three years. Do you really think you're over him after just a few days?" She has a valid point, one I've said to myself over and over again when thinking about Ian.

"Does it make me a bitch to say I wasn't that sad when I found out he was cheating?" Jade gives me a look of derision, and I smile. "Okay, fine, at first I was hurt obviously. But once I thought about my relationship with him, I realized we were drifting apart, and in the end, being away from him is the best thing since he can't keep himself to one woman."

Jade eyes me curiously. "So what, you were just with him for that long because the sex was good?" she jokes, but a look of caution replaces her smile, and I take a breath, readying myself for what I'm about to confess.

"The sex was awful," I admit, her eyes bulging as I take a sip of my drink. "At first, it was great. We were all over each other and couldn't go a few days without ending up in bed. But after about a year, I wanted more."

She eyes me again, curious. "What do you mean you wanted more, like volume?"

I laugh, shaking my head. "No, I wanted more

intensity, more variety, and Brad refused to change. So our sex life tanked after that."

"I can see why you guys drifted apart," she says somberly. I nod, knowing that finding out he was a cheating bastard was the best thing to ever happen to me. Even if I never met Ian.

"So," Jade inquires after the server leaves, "are you going to the bar?" I've thought about this for the past few days, and the more time that passes, the more I want to see him. The more I try to push the thought of him out of my head, the more time he spends there. So I know I have to see where this goes.

"Yeah, I am." She shakes her head, taking a sip of her mimosa as if she knows how this is going to end. But for me, this is the start of something new and exciting, and I can't wait to see him tonight.

The second the bar door shuts behind me and I lock eyes with Ian, I know I've made the right choice. He yells to his partner that he's taking a break, and before I can say a word, his fingers are laced with mine as he pulls me down a dark hallway and into a room that looks like an office.

I open my mouth to ask what he's doing, but I don't have the chance to utter a word. His mouth is on mine, and his hands find the edge of my skirt. Did I wear this outfit on purpose, hoping this would happen? Maybe? All I can say is that I'm glad I did because the feel of his calloused fingers against my inner thigh is causing my brain to short-circuit.

"Goddamn, I thought I embellished how good you tasted, but *fuck*, my memory didn't do you justice." I groan, my hips circling, wanting more than what he's giving me. "You have no idea how many hours I've spent watching that front door," he admits, and my heart stutters, liking that confession a little too much.

"Ian," I whisper, my fingers tugging at the hair on the back of his neck, wanting his lips, but he shakes his head as he ignores my pleas and kisses down my neck. "Please..." He shakes his head again as his eyes lift to mine. The hunger I see gazing back at me causes wetness to pool between my legs, and when I cross my legs, needing some kind of friction, he smirks.

"Nope, none of that," he murmurs, taking my knees and spreading them apart before taking both my wrists in one of his hands and lifting them above my head. My intake of breath takes us both off guard, and something unlocks inside my brain. "You like that, don't you, baby?" he whispers against the shell of my ear, nipping at the lobe as his fingers tighten on my wrists. I nod because being restrained is something I've thought about but never tried, and *fucking hell,* is it turning me on.

"Ian?" My uncertainty is clear as his eyes soften and he kisses me lightly.

"You like the idea of being restrained? Was that something you wanted to try and couldn't?" He doesn't say why, but we both know the answer before I nod. "Fucking sexy as hell," he mutters before kissing me one more time. "I want you to keep those hands right there for me, okay? No moving." I nod, his eyes darkening. "Good girl."

"*Shit,*" I moan, my hips circling because those two words cause an inferno to light within me.

"*Interesting.* We will definitely be coming back to that. But for now, I want to see how you taste." And before I can say a word, Ian sinks to his knees and pushes up my skirt. Within a second, his tongue dips through my dripping-wet folds, and I'm lost.

It doesn't take long before he has me on edge, but just when I'm about to fall over, my hand grasps his hair, and he stops instantly. My eyes fall to his in a panic, my chest heaving as that smirk plays on the edge of his lips. I know exactly what he's about to say.

"I told you to keep those hands above your head. Only good girls who listen get rewarded." My head thumps against the wooden door behind me as I close my eyes and lift my hands once more, grasping the trim around the door for support. "That's a good girl. Keep them right there." I groan, my legs giving out as his tongue continues its ministrations, taking me over the edge in rapid succession. Before I know it, his fingers join the party, plunging inside my wet heat, and soon, I'm cresting over the hill once more, screaming his name.

CHAPTER 5

Ian

The taste of her still lingers on my lips as I place the plate of food in front of her, and I know that this "benefits arrangement" we have going on will burn me hard. The longer I spend with her, the more I want to know and the more I want to taste, and that's a deadly combination for a guy who could get burned at the end of this. As she devours her meal, I take a moment to really take her in. And not for the first time tonight, I wonder where she's been all my life.

"You need to stop staring at me like that. You're going to give me a complex." I smirk, loving the color that dusts her cheeks and nose. I wasn't lying when I told her I'd been watching the front door for days because meeting her rocked the foundation I thought was solid beneath my feet, but it turns out it crumbled with one look from her gorgeous blue eyes.

"Maybe that's what you deserve," I whisper, taking her lips in a soft kiss before walking away to serve more drinks. Once we were done in my office, we both righted ourselves, and I asked her to stay until my shift ended. She shyly said yes just as her stomach rumbled loudly, and I knew I needed to get some food into her. I wanted to fill her with so much more than food, but I vowed when I dropped her off at home that I would let her decide how far this goes and how fast. Yet after tonight, that might be a bit harder to stand behind.

"So..." she says, clearing her throat. Her eyes dart around the room, and I smile at her avoidance of my gaze. "What made you buy this place?" I place both hands on the bar and lean forward, my eyes taking in everything around us and trying to see it from her perspective.

"You're not the first one to think I don't fit in here, your ex included." Her eyes darken at the mention of her ex, but she shakes her head, shoving aside her plate and holding my gaze.

"That's not what I meant. It never occurred to me that you might not fit in here." I tilt my head, not believing her, and I open my mouth to say just that, but she continues before I can get a word in. "What I meant was, you seem young to own a bar."

"I came into an inheritance when I turned eighteen and never had the desire to go to college. I wanted to make something of myself, so I found this place and bought it." Her eyes linger on my lips, and I wonder if anything I just said bothered her, so I ask.

"Why would any of that bother me?"

"Most people have that reaction when I say I never went to college. Most of the clientele here spent hundreds of thousands of dollars to make the money they do, and they always assume I don't know what I'm doing because I don't have a degree." I half expected her to agree with the statement, but she burst out laughing.

"I hate to break it to you, but most of the men who come in here put on a facade of success when, in reality, they're probably jealous of your independence and the fact that you work for yourself." I stand there stunned because that was the last thing I expected to come out of her mouth.

"You're pretty amazing. You know that, right?" I whisper, leaning over the bar and taking her lips with mine, wanting so much to take it deeper but knowing with prying eyes all around us, we can't.

"I know. I didn't go to college either, and I'm

mildly successful in my field." She winks, and I chuckle softly as I stand and take her hand in mine. "Before you ask, yes, my parents hated it, but they got over it once they realized how happy I was to be outside of a stuffy classroom and following my passion."

"What do you do, if you don't mind me asking?" She smiles shyly as her eyes dart everywhere but mine. "You don't have to answer, you know." She shakes her head, releasing my hand.

"No, it's fine. It's just that no one has really asked me about what I do before." I eye her and wonder why but she continues to talk before I can ask. "I'm a writer." I smile, knowing that career fits her perfectly.

"What kind of things do you write?"

"Mostly fantasy and science fiction romance novels." Her cheeks redden at the admission, and I tilt my head to the side.

"Are you embarrassed about that?" She shrugs, taking another sip of her drink.

"Honestly, most people have an opinion when I tell them. Brad always told me I should write real fiction since my work was just fluff." My fingers clench into fists at the thought of punching that douchebag so hard his family feels it. "But he never knew how much I made from it, so it's his loss." Her look of hesitancy tells me that she expects me to ask her how much she makes, but I couldn't care less. There's something else I want to know more.

"What are you doing this weekend?" I ask, taking a breath because I have no idea how this will go down.

"Free as a bird." She smiles, interlocking our fingers. "Why, you wanna take me on a date?" she teases.

"Something like that. I want to take you somewhere." Her brow furrows, and it's the cutest thing I've ever seen.

"That's a bit cryptic, you know." I nod, knowing how it sounds, but I don't want to scare her just yet. When I don't elaborate, she continues, "You're really not going to tell me?" I shake my head, hoping to God she trusts me enough to let me do this for her. "Fine. You win." I smile, my chest expanding because this girl is everything I want, and if I have it my way, she'll be mine by the end of the weekend.

CHAPTER 6
Halley

T*ext me when you get here.* That's all Ian's message says as I walk down the street to the address he texted me last night. He still wouldn't tell me what this place was or what to expect from the night. But standing here and peering up at what seems to be a regular house has me a bit perplexed. I take out my phone and send Ian a quick message, and before I have the chance to put my phone away, the front door opens, and Ian walks out, looking sinful in all black.

"Hey, baby," he mutters before taking my lips, his hand finding the small of my back and pulling me even closer. I try not to think much about the nickname, knowing this is only temporary. But I love it all the same.

"What is this place?" A flicker of uncertainty enters his gaze, and I wonder if I made a mistake in coming here. I mean, technically, I don't know much about Ian. I've only known him a week, and I've already let him eat me out like it was his last meal. Before I can think too much, he kisses me once more and takes my hand, leading me toward the front door.

"This is a sex club."

I choke on nothing, my feet planting because I couldn't have heard him properly. "Excuse me...what?"

He chuckles softly as he takes my face in the palm of his hands, bringing my eyes to his. "Take a breath for me, okay?" he whispers, and I do as he says, the panic of what lies beyond those doors dissipating slowly. "I want you to know that you are not obligated to do anything in there, okay? That's not why I brought you here."

"Then why did you?" I question, not understanding why he would think this was the next logical step after what we shared in his office.

"Because from what I've seen, I think you'll enjoy it. Delirium is a club for people to explore themselves, either alone or with a partner. No one is here against their will, and I promise if you hate it, we will leave immediately." I nod because a secret part of me always wanted to come here. It's been discussed around me for years, but I've never had the courage to ask more about it. But now, the opportunity to see it causes a fire to light deep within me, and I want to see what all the fuss is about.

"What made you think of bringing me here?" I wonder aloud as he fist-bumps the bodyguard at the front door. "Like specifically?" I elaborate.

"When I held your hands above your head the other night, you liked that, right?" I nod, hating the way the blush colors my cheeks. "Well, being restrained is a kind of kink that can be explored here." My heart rate picks up. The idea of being left at his mercy causes my palms to sweat and wetness to pool between my legs. "And let's not forget your praise kink." I stop walking again, my mouth hanging open. "What? When I called you a good girl, you flooded my mouth. You can't deny that. Baby, you loved it." Fucking hell, he's right.

Neither of us says a word as Ian leads me farther into the club, my eyes taking in everything and nothing all at once. It's not until we pass through a teal velvet curtain that my eyes bug out of their sockets, and my mouth drops open. I don't know what I expected a sex club to look like, but it wasn't this. The room is huge, filled with couches, chairs, and beds along almost every wall. As my eyes cast upward, I realize every room on the second floor has a glass wall, allowing everyone on the first floor to see every detail of what's happening behind those closed doors.

I take a shuddering breath as my gaze filters down to one of the beds where a man finishes restraining a woman to the headboard by her hands. My labored breathing causes me to become light-headed as a need I never knew was inside me comes roaring to the surface.

I want that. I want that more than I knew.

"I see you've found something interesting to watch," Ian murmurs into my ear as I grin, feeling the heat creep through my body as he pulls me flush against his body. My head turns, but before I can take his lips with mine like I planned, his fingers grip the edge of my jaw and hold my face forward. "Don't take your eyes off them, okay?" I nod my head as his hands slide over my body, teasing over the low waist of my skirt. In front of us, the man tightens the straps that bind her, stretching her arms up above her head. Her legs are spread as the man crawls between them, his eyes focused and his mouth intent on tasting her. That's when I feel the adrenaline and excitement charge through me. Her moans crest loudly the second his tongue touches her skin as her fingers pull on the bonds that hold her in place.

Ian's fingers slip beneath the edge of my skirt,

finding the lace of my panties, and before I take a breath, his fingers swirl over my clit, causing my head to fall back onto his chest. "Dirty girl...is this turning you on?" he whispers into my ear, and I only nod because I can't take my eyes off the couple in front of us. "Is that what you want, baby?" he asks, his fingers dipping farther and farther inside me as my knees begin to give out. "You want me to take you while you have no choice but to take it?" I'm nodding before the words even register in my brain because I just want the ache inside me to go away.

Before I can beg him to take me somewhere, he spins me around and leads me into one of the closed-off rooms down a darkened hall, pushing me up against a wall just as the door shuts behind us. I open my mouth as a panicked feeling enters my brain, not wanting anyone to see me like this. But Ian kisses me, devouring my mouth before my brain can go into overdrive.

"No one will ever see you come but me. This is a private room." I nod, lacing my fingers in his hair and pulling his mouth back to mine, but before I bask in the feel of the loose strands, my wrists are hauled above my head and restrained in leather cuffs.

"Ian," I moan, my head falling back against the wall, my hips searching. He takes no time stripping me from the waist down, my eyes taking him in as he undoes his jeans and shoves them to the floor, my mouth watering at the sight of his cock and wanting nothing more than to know what it feels like to have it plunge inside me.

"You have no fucking idea how beautiful you look right now," he mumbles as he takes out a condom, rolls it down his impressive length, and steps into me, his lips taking mine as he lifts my legs to wrap them around his waist. "Fuck, baby," he groans as I whimper, kissing him even harder. No one has ever made me this out of my mind with lust, and I want more. So much more.

I expect him to fuck me right then and there, but instead, he rips open my top, taking one of my nipples in his mouth, causing a moan to escape my throat. "Ian, please...I need..." His lips take mine once before sliding down my neck, leaving small bite marks across my skin.

"Tell me, baby," he purrs. "Tell me what you want, Halley."

"You," I whisper. "I need you to fuck me." He groans, crushing his lips to mine just as he places his cock at my entrance and surges inside me in one long and hard stroke. Pulling on my restraints creates a bite of pain that causes my walls to clamp down around his hard cock that is now pulsing inside me.

"*Goddamn*, Halley," he groans, kissing me through our panting breaths. "Jesus, you are so fucking tight." My head falls back against the wall, and I start begging incoherently because the feel of him inside me is unlike anything I have ever experienced. I love sex. I've had some great experiences in my life, but this? This is on another level altogether.

With a grunt, Ian wraps his hand around my neck, then lightly trails down between my breasts before gripping my hips and holding me still against the wall as he fucks me hard. "Ian!" I cry out in pure ecstasy, seeing stars as he starts to slide in and out of me, grinding his cock as deep as he possibly can while a new wave of pleasure starts to drown me. My legs cling to him as I gasp, melting as the orgasm crests, and I explode. Ian sinks deep into my clenching pussy, and I come *hard* just as Ian stills inside me, finding his own ecstasy.

"You are...," he starts but doesn't finish as he takes my lips in a sweet, gentle kiss that sends a whole new wave of emotions coursing through my body. His gaze meets mine, and I swear I see the same longing mirrored back at me. Before I can comment on it, it's gone, and Ian rests his head on my still exposed chest.

"You were right. This was a good idea." I say as a shiver racks my body, causing Ian to laugh deep within his chest. But in reality, at this moment, Ian made me fall for him more than I already was, and I couldn't figure out if that was a good thing or the worst idea I've ever had.

CHAPTER 7

Ian

It's been three weeks of bliss. Three weeks of Halley coming into the bar most nights to hang out, and three weeks of us going into Delirium on Friday nights and sometimes Saturdays, depending on our mood. Three weeks of me slowly falling for the woman, even though I know she only wants to be friends with benefits. I know this. We've talked about it, and I understand she's not ready for a relationship. I get it, but it doesn't stop the way my heart stops every time she walks into a room or how my body reacts when she makes those noises when I'm inside her.

But the longer I spend with Halley, the more I know I have to end it. I can't go on pretending I'm not falling in love with her. I can't pretend that being with her isn't the best part of my day. I just can't. So when the front door of the bar opens, and my eyes connect with hers, I take a deep breath, hating what I'm about to do.

"Why do you look like someone ran over your dog?" Halley asks. Sitting in her usual spot, she crooks her finger before leaning over the bar and taking my lips in a sweet but scarce kiss. "And why are you kissing me like I'm your sister and not the woman you fuck every Friday night?" I roll my eyes, trying to laugh it off as I walk away and head toward the kitchen to get her food. Once I'm out of view, I lean against the hallway wall and close my eyes. My head hits the drywall as I second-guess why I'm doing this.

"What is going on with you?" Halley asks as I set the food in front of her. I expect her to dig in like she does every other night she's here, but instead, her eyes bore into mine, and I panic.

"Nothing's wrong. I'm just tired." It's not a total lie. I am tired, but the reason has everything to do with her and the fact that I want her every day for the rest of my life. Halley tilts her head, her eyes questioning me, and I can see the moment she chooses to believe me, even though I know she doesn't. I try to ignore her eyes as they follow me as I work, filling drinks, cleaning the bar, and stocking the liquor behind me. But over time, the stone in the pit of my stomach begins to grow enough that I know if I don't say something soon, I might never do it.

"So, are we on for the club tomorrow?" she asks, taking a bite out of her standard chicken fingers and fries, a dish I used to make fun of her for but now find endearing. Her question slowly registers, and I know it's now or never, so I shake my head.

"No, I don't think so." My voice is hushed, and for a second, I wonder if she didn't hear me, but then my eyes meet hers, and I see the hurt and confusion staring back at me.

"What do you mean, no? Why don't you want to go?" Her voice cracks, and I watch as her eyes fall, the uncertainty clear in her gaze.

"Look," I start, hating every second of this. "I don't think we should see each other anymore." There. Like a Band-Aid, I ripped it off in one motion, but now I'm left with the open wound.

"What?" she whispers, her voice breaking, and I swear my heart breaks a little at the sound. "What do you mean? I thought..." She doesn't finish the thought. I open my mouth to explain myself, but she shakes her head. The tears threaten to fall from her eyes, but my girl is strong, and she pushes them back.

"Halley," I start, but she holds up her hand.

"You know what? I'm sick and tired of men

playing with my emotions. God, I can't believe I thought..." She stops, and my heart stops with her. Could she want more too?

"You thought what?" I question, my hands shaking as I white-knuckle the edge of the bar. "Halley, you're the one who told me you only wanted benefits. That you couldn't do more than that." Silence deafens the bar as I wait for her to answer. When she doesn't, I hop over the bar and take her face in the palm of my hands. "Halley, what do you want?" I ask, needing the words before I get my hopes up.

At first, she says nothing, her eyes darting back and forth between mine, and I wonder if I misread her. Maybe she's just pissed she's not going to get some every week. But then her teary eyes meet mine, and her shaking hands clasp around mine that are gently holding the base of her throat.

"I want more," she whispers, her gaze dropping to the floor, and I take a shuddering breath. "I know I said all I wanted was benefits, but now...now I want more. I want it all. With you." The tears fall freely now, and I wipe them away with the pads of my thumb. "I tried not to fall for you. I tried so hard, but you wormed your way inside my heart, and now I can't get you out." I smile, lifting her chin with my thumbs so her eyes meet mine before I lower my lips to hers.

"*Fucking hell*, you have no idea how insanely happy I am to hear those words," I murmur against her lips. Just as I try to take the kiss deeper, she pushes me away, and I stumble back in shock.

"What the hell, Ian? A second ago, you were breaking up with me." I can't help it when I laugh. Halley shoots daggers my way, and I try to suppress my laughter as best as I can before walking toward her once more.

"Baby, I was only doing that because I'm falling head over heels for you and couldn't stand only being your friend with benefits." Her eyes widen as I smile, taking her lips in a kiss that shows her just how much I want her.

"Are you serious right now?" I nod, leaning my forehead against hers. "You know that's pretty fucked up," she teases. I take her lips once more, loving the way her body fits against mine.

"But you're mine now, right? No more of that other bullshit. I want you, Halley. I want your laughs, your smiles, and your love. I want it all." She smiles, taking my lips in a kiss that shows me exactly how in sync we are, and I thank the stars that she walked into my life when she did because she's turned it upside down, and I couldn't ask for anything more.

Want a Free book?

Join my newsletter and get a FREE copy of my short story Wounded Hearts! Download HERE

Acknowledgments

Thank you to my husband, who has stood by me throughout this journey. I know I can be hard to handle when deadlines hit, but your love and support will always mean the world to me.

Thank you to my family for supporting me no matter what I chose to do. They have always known that writing is my passion and seeing their support for that passion means everything to me.

Thank you to my BETA and ARC teams for reading my very rough drafts and telling me straight up what I need to change and how to create a better story. Thank you for sharing, loving and promoting my work. Without you, there would be no books to read and for that I am eternally grateful.

Thank you to Ellie at My Brothers Editor. Thank you for taking me on, thank you for supporting me the way you have these past few months and thank you for elevating my work, it wouldn't be where it is today without you.

To my readers. When I started this journey, I didn't

know what to expect, and the level of love and support I've garnered over the last year has been something I never expected. You are the reason I do this job. You are the reason I write the stories I do, because you devour them and love them as much as I do. I hope that never changes.

About the Author

S.A. Clayton lives in a small town outside of Toronto, Canada with her husband and her scary large collection of books that seem to take over every room.

She has worked on both sides of the publishing industry, both in a bookstore and for actual publishing companies. Although she loved both for different reasons, she found that writing was her true passion and has spent the last few years breaking into the industry as best she can.

She is a lover of all things romance and began her writing journey in her late twenties. Since then, she has immersed herself in the romance genre and couldn't be happier.

When she's not writing or reading, she enjoys binging a great Netflix show (Stranger Things anyone?), baking (because who doesn't love cookies!) and spending time with her family.

Also by S.A Clayton

Standalone's

Wrapped Up in You

Tangled Up in You

Sweet Valentine

Holiday Hookup

Forbidden CEO

Unauthorized Behaviour

Pick Six

Easy to Lose

Tempting Fate

Tempting You

In Plain Sight

Because You're Mine

Lucky Charm

Stadium Series

Hardball

Curveball

Fastball

Harbour Cove Series

Hoping for Her

Falling for Her

Waiting for Her

Staying for Her

Perfect for Her